# The Al Anbar Chronicles

# PRISONER OF FALLUJAH

Colonel Jonathan P. Brazee, USMCR (Ret)

Semper Fi Press

A Semper Fi Press Book

May 2013


Copyright © 2013 by Jonathan Brazee

ISBN-13: 978-0615814254
ISBN-10: 0615814255


Printed in the United States of America

Acknowledgements:

I want to thank all those who took the time to pre-read this book, catching my mistakes in both content and typing. From VFW Post 9951 in Bangkok, I need to thank MacAlan Thompson for his proofreading and fact-checking. From the KDP Author's forum, I want to thank Nick Stephenson and Robert Coleman for making sure by "Brit-speak" rang true. And most of all, thanks to my editor, Gabriella West, for keeping me on the straight and narrow. All remaining typos and inaccuracies are solely my fault.

Cover Photography by Jonathan Brazee

# Chapter 1

*February 28, 2006*
*Fallujah, Iraq*

I pulled the edge of my hood out an inch, trying to get some air to circulate. It was only February, but Fallujah was already an oven. Wearing my uniform, gloves, body armor, a hood, all my battle gear, and goggles didn't help, and the Humvee's small air conditioner couldn't keep up with the heat.

We were on our orientation convoy, our first in Iraq, getting ready for when the main body started arriving in a week. I really wasn't too concerned. This was my third pump. My first two were as a grunt, so this one, on glorified convoy duty, should be a breeze. This was just an easy route out the gates, around the open area surrounding the camp, and a quick jaunt into the outskirts of the town itself. We'd done about a million convoys back at Pendleton during weekend drills and again after we mobilized, but the powers that be decided that we still had to get certified in-country before we could perform a real mission.

I glanced down at my watch, trying to make the calculations. I hit LCpl Deke Miller in the leg to get his attention. He looked down at me from his position in the gun turret.

"Hey, Miller, what time's it back in California?"

He glanced at his watch and without a pause replied, "9:30 PM" before looking back up, scanning for any sign of the enemy.

I felt a twinge of guilt. This wasn't Pendleton. There were bad guys out there, and I shouldn't be pulling our gunner's attention off his mission.

Nine-thirty. Sig would have gotten off work 30 minutes ago. I wondered if she was already home. I hadn't heard anything from her since the buses left Pendleton for March AFB and the long flight to Kuwait. No e-mails at all. I had tried to call her from the USO at Camp Liberty while getting processed to proceed into Iraq, but she never picked up. I knew she was pissed about this deployment, but this was taking it too far. This was her way of punishing me, just like her refusing one last fuck before I left, and I'd just have to wait for her to cool off.

I tried to put her out of my mind and looked out the window. I was riding in the right rear seat of the Humvee, essentially a passenger with no real mission other than to observe. Outside the window, the mostly featureless desert stretched to the south, and the buildings of Fallujah rose miragelike off to the west. It was a tight fit with all my battle gear, and I didn't like riding with my knees so high, even higher than my hips. I never did like this aspect of the configuration of a Hummer with the low seat and the high floorboard. It didn't feel particularly safe to me if we were hit or had an accident.

This Hummer was the up-armored variant, carrying about 1,000 pounds of extra protection, so at least that was an improvement on what we had on my previous two pumps. There were rumors of a new vehicle with a v-shaped bottom coming, but they wouldn't get in theater until long after we were back in the US and de-mobilized.

Up ahead, I could see the lead vehicle take a right as we turned towards Fallujah. We had six Hummers and a 5-ton in the convoy. I had ridden a 5-ton from Kuwait to Baghdad back in 2003 when I was a grunt with 3/4, the "Thundering Third," and, frankly, I was glad that I had at least the cushioned seat of the Hummer to sit on. A 5-ton was pretty hard on the body, even if it put a lot of steel between you and any IED.

Dust devils danced across the sand as we all made the turn and headed into Fallujah. We were not going to go very far into the city: just up to near the government compound, then hang a right and come back to camp. This convoy was merely to get our feet wet before we were given a real mission. Conducting a convoy back in Pendleton was one thing. Conducting one where the enemy was a very real threat was something else.

Most of the Marines in the battery were pretty disgusted with our assignment. We would not be firing any tubes during our deployment. We were assigned as a provisional MP company, taking police-type duties. It didn't bother me none. I was still an 0311, a grunt. I just joined the battery in November, when they were already in their work-ups, and I had never even trained as an artilleryman yet. An active duty battery would be providing all the arty fire support, but as reservists, most of us were on convoy duty, which made sense given all the drivers a battery has. It takes a shitload of trucks to move around a battery's guns and ammo.

The radio crackled with instructions to keep it tight, but watch our dispersion. Staff Sergeant Rios was our vehicle commander, and he just rolled his head in exaggerated wonder. I'm not sure how we could keep it tight and disbursed at the same time, and he evidently felt the same.

I looked over the hump running down the middle of the Hummer to the passenger in the back left seat. The chaplain had insisted on coming. He looked pretty nervous, but I had to give him credit for coming out with us. You can't lead a flock from behind. Maybe having him there would give us a little extra protection from the big man upstairs.

As we pulled into the built-up area, I paid more attention to what was around us. It wasn't as if I could engage anyone if we got hit. Our windows didn't lower, and we didn't have any sort of gun port. No, that would be up to Miller on the .50. But this was my first glimpse of Fallujah, and from all reports, the fighting had been pretty fierce here back in 2004. I was in-country at the time of the Battle of Fallujah, but not here.

I was a bit disappointed that it looked like every other dusty Iraqi town I'd seen. There was some damage evident, but not like the photos of destruction in Japan and Germany from back in

WWII. I'm not sure what I expected, but certainly something more dramatic than this.

As I was looking out the window, we started to drift a bit to my side of the road. In all our rehearsals, we had it drilled into our heads to keep our vehicle tracks in the ones of the vehicles ahead of us. Not three hours ago, in our convoy brief, the battalion S-3 had stressed the same thing. And here we were starting to make our own way. I looked up at SSgt Rios, wondering if he was going to tell LCpl Morrisey, our driver, to fall back in trace of the Hummer in front of us. I hesitated a moment; I was new to the battery, and Rios was a SNCO. I was just a corporal.

We drifted another foot or so, and I knew I had to say something. I released my seatbelt and leaned forward, head over my knees, just as SSgt Rios seemed to realize that we had drifted. He turned to Morrisey, so I settled back into my seat.

The instant my back touched the back of my seat, the world erupted with a roar. I felt like a giant had hit my seat, throwing the Hummer, and me with it, up in the air. I felt a flash of heat, almost too intense to bear. Stunned, I really didn't know what had happened for a moment, but then it struck me. We'd been hit by an IED.

The Hummer was airborne, but canted so the right side was above the left, and I hung half in and half out of the vehicle, suspended over the dusty road. We'd been briefed that the Hummer's doors often got stuck when the vehicle hit an IED, but my door had been torn right off. I glanced over to see the chaplain holding on for dear life while Miller's legs flailed in the air inside the Hummer, his torso still out of the gun turret hatch.

All of this couldn't have taken more than two seconds, but time seemed suspended to me. Life had gone into super-slow-mo mode. Up we went, then the Hummer started its unstoppable plunge back down to earth. I braced myself, but it didn't do much good. The vehicle hit hard on its left side. It stopped cold, but I didn't. I tumbled over and out to slam on the ground, my breath knocked out of me. I looked up, seeing the remnants of the black smoke from the explosion disburse into the blue sky above me, then the tottering Humvee looking like it was trying to decide which way to fall. I could see this, and I realized that if it fell on me, I was a goner. But this was almost an unemotional acknowledgment. I knew it would crush me, but I didn't feel a sense of panic. If it crushed me, it crushed me. I certainly could not move out of the way in time.

After an eternity, the Hummer fell over—to the left. I was in the clear. Still dazed, I heard the sound of small arms, the distinctive chatter of AK-47s, but as if through cotton being stuffed in my ears. This registered on me, but without a sense of urgency. The .50s in the other vehicles opened up in reply, and I could see tracers painting lines across the street and into one of the adjacent buildings.

It took an effort, but I managed to sit up. I stared stupidly at the wreck of a Hummer lying upside down next to me. The left hand rear door opened, and out tumbled the chaplain, who then reached back in to help Miller out. LCpl Miller had leaned back in to help Morrisey out when someone took a sledgehammer and hit me in the chest. I fell to my back and struggled to breathe. I knew I had been shot, and the weird complacency I had been feeling vanished. I was going to die here, a million miles away from home, on a hot dusty street in Fallujah. Two tours as a grunt without a scratch, and I buy it as an arty-slash-MP?

I managed to reach to my chest with my left hand, then I brought it up to my line of sight, expecting to see my blood staining it red. The glove on my hand looked scorched, but it was not red. I wondered what that meant, but tunnel vision crept in and all went dark.

# Chapter 2

*Same Day*
*Camp Fallujah Hospital*

I hurt.

All over.

My butt hurt, my back hurt. My lips hurt. It hurt to breathe, each breath sending lances of pain through my chest.

"How're you feeling, son?" a calm voice asked me.

I opened my eyes to see the chaplain sitting on a chair beside me. He was filthy, covered with soot and dust. He looked OK, though. I realized I didn't even know his name, or what kind of chaplain he was.

"Am I OK?" I asked.

I looked around. How come no doctors were treating me? I'd been shot!

"You'll be fine, Cpl Xenakis, isn't it?  Can I call you Nicholas? I don't think we've officially met yet. I'm Father Trent."

"Just Nick's fine, Father," I answered.

He held out his hand as if we were casually meeting back at Seal Beach. By instinct, I took it, but that brought another stab of pain in my chest. I had been stripped and somewhat cleaned up, so it was easy to lift up the sheet over me and look at my chest. An angry red welt now adorned my right pec.

"Yes, the doctor said you're going to have a pretty serious bruise there, but your flak jacket stopped the round itself. You'll need an x-ray, but he doesn't think you broke a rib or anything."

"But, why'd I, I mean why'd I..."

"Pass out? Well, you need to ask the doc, but I think he said you've got a concussion. The IED was right underneath you when it went off."

I looked around, but the other beds were empty.

"Is everyone OK?"

Father Trent's eyes clouded over a bit before he answered. "LCpl Miller was shot in the arm, and he's in surgery now. He was pulling you back out of the line of fire when he was hit. He's going to pull through, they said, but he could lose the arm."

I felt a pang of guilt. Miller was one of the Marines in the battery that I knew the best. We both lived in Westminster (best known for its "Little Saigon"), and he was a former grunt, too. He was using the GI Bill and his drill pay to support himself while he was taking classes at Coastline Community College.

"I see you're awake. You feeling OK now?" A corpsman had walked up while I was talking to the chaplain.

"Not too good, to be honest."

The corpsman gave a rueful laugh. "Yeah, I would imagine so. You're going to be pretty sore for a few days. None of that's too serious, but you've got a concussion, and we're going to keep you overnight for observation. If you're feeling up to it, let's get you cleaned up, and Doctor Whipple's ordered a chest x-ray, just to be on the safe side."

He turned to Father Trent. "You might as well get cleaned up, too, sir. I'll take care of Xenakis here now."

Father Trent looked at me, obviously torn.

"You go, sir. Get cleaned up. When LCpl Miller's out of surgery, he might need you," I told him.

That seemed to register, because he got up, wished me well, and left, but not before promising to be back to check up on me.

"We kept your first sergeant and the rest out, but the chaplain, he insisted on staying until you woke up. Well, let's get going," he said, as he brought a wheelchair up to the bed.

I started to protest, but that didn't do me any good.

"Sorry there, corporal. But you've taken a knock on the head, and regs are regs. You get yours truly as your personal chauffeur. And here, you might want more of this," he told me, handing me a white tube of cream.

I took it, then looked at him questioningly.

"For your lips. You got burned there, where you weren't covered up. Your gear saved you from being burnt anywhere else.

We kept your gear after we took it off you. Most of it can't be used anymore, but it might make a good souvenir."

I eased off the bed and into the chair. I was hurting more than after any football game back at high school. I felt a little conspicuous having a grown man push me in a chair, but it was probably better than me trying to walk to the shower. I'd hate to try it only to fall on my ass and have to get someone to help me up.

## Chapter 3

*March 21, 2006*
*Camp Fallujah, Iraq*

"Hey Xenakis, get back to the battery. We've got a mission."

I looked up from my burger at Sgt Jones. I had just sat down to chow, and the burgers were really pretty good. All of the food was good, to be honest, and I was eating better than I ate back home. We even got prime rib every Sunday, if you could believe that. Iraq in 2006 was much different from my two previous pumps, and the food was a welcome change for the better.

"Now, Xenakis, and get everyone else together," Jones said as I hesitated.

"OK, OK, I'm coming."

I stood up, and as he turned away, I took two huge bites of the burger, ketchup and mayo running out onto my chin. I wiped my chin with my sleeve and hurried out of the DFAC. I wondered what was so important. We didn't have a convoy scheduled for today. Other MP's had PTT duty, and that was pretty much a 24/7 assignment, but with the loyalties of the Iraqi police questionable, I was glad we did convoy escorts rather than being on a Police Transition Team. That duty went to the active duty MP company, anyway.

The heat hit me as I left the air conditioning and made my way to the battery office. We were an MP company now, but everyone still referred to us as a battery, so who was I to argue? I entered the hatch, eyes taking a moment to adjust from the bright Iraqi sun.

"Into the briefing room, Xenakis," Gunny Pancoast told me.

I nodded and went inside the small room and took a seat. Most of the other platoon NCOs were already there. The room was pretty rough. None of the plywood walls or work benches had been finished, and cables snaked every-which-way connecting computers, lights, and what have you. I asked Cpl Kim what was up, but he hadn't a clue, so I sat back to wait for the lieutenant.

I leaned back and stretched, and a twinge in my chest reminded me of the bruise there that had by now faded to a sickly shade of yellow. For awhile there, the other Marines in the unit had called it my "purple heart," one the Corps couldn't take away. I had to admit that despite it being on my right side rather than my left, the bruise did sort of look like a dark purple heart. My ass had also been pretty bruised, but I was glad that no nickname had arisen due to that one. I could just imagine what they might have come up with.

I thought of my uneaten burger. Typical Corps, hurry up and wait. I would've had time to eat the burger and even make a trip to the ice cream bar.

Finally, Lieutenant Richmond and Gunny Templeton walked in. We came to attention, then took our seats. The lieutenant was one of the few lieutenants in the battery. Other platoon commander billets, which were T/O'd for lieutenants, were filled by captains who had already served their active duty tours. 1stLt Richmond had done three years on active duty, all at Kaneohe Bay, as a supply officer. Now, as a reservist, he finally made it to the Sandbox. He seemed pretty capable, for all of that.

"Take your seats, gentlemen," he told us. He was rather fond of the term "gentlemen." We were Marines, though, not gentlemen. Maybe he was, at least by an act of Congress, but we sure weren't.

"We've got ourselves a little extra mission for the day. Nothing too big, but we take what we can get. As you know, violence has increased as a result of the bombing of the Golden Mosque. Most of this is Shiite/Sunni. We haven't been too affected by this yet, but the Army has conducted several operations like *Swarmer* last week."

*Operation Swarmer* was a huge airborne operation, suitably covered by CNN and Fox, who called it the biggest airborne operation since Vietnam. Word on the street was that it was pretty much a big dog-and-pony show.

"Well, they also pulled off *Operation Swamp Fox*, capturing over 100 insurgents, and some of MNF-West's ITT teams and MPs have gone over to supplement them. With them gone, we're a little short-handed, and the grunts in town have captured our own insurgents. We've been tasked with providing the processing for the EPWs until ITT can do their thing. I want two teams ready to go as soon as they bring in the EPWs from the government compound. SSgt Cordero will be in charge, but I want everyone standing by in case they're needed."

Our primary duty was convoy escort, but we'd had training on handling Enemy Prisoners of War, mostly in the collection points and holding areas. We had, though spent a day on a mock processing center. I hoped we'd be doing the former rather than the latter. All those things like fingerprinting, clothing issue, haircuts, photos, and such ran together in my mind. I wasn't sure that any of us really knew how to set one of those up. It was one thing to designate us as an MP company, but it was another for us to actually know how to do everything a real 5811 did.

The lieutenant left to get more information, and the gunny told SSgt Cordero who he had. I was one of those chosen. As a former grunt, I guess they thought I would be somehow better qualified for tasks that required standing around with my M16. I was used to it, though. Krispen Craig was also selected. Cpl Craig was an active duty 5811, a real military policeman, before he became a reservist and joined the battery. Truth be told, though, I thought most of us knew more about our new duties than "Krispy Kreme." He wasn't the brightest bulb in the pack.

Like most reserve units, we were a bit heavy in NCOs and lacking in lance corporals and below. We did have some, though, and SSgt Cordero sent us off to get those assigned to the mission. I grabbed LCpl Fowler just as he left the DFAC, ketchup staining the collar of his utilities blouse. At least he had gotten to eat first. I told him to go change and meet us in front of the company office.

By the time we are all gathered there, Gunny Pancoast had more info, and he went with us to the EPW holding area, thank goodness. We were just going to be guarding them, not processing them. We waited around for about 30 minutes when a 5-ton truck, escorted by two gun Hummers, drove up. A PTT sergeant got out of the lead Hummer and sauntered over. Gunny Pancoast was still with us, and the sergeant ignored us to speak to the gunny. To me, he seemed a bit arrogant. I thought the active duty MPs sometimes treated us with a bit of a condescending manner, and even if I was on active duty only a few months ago, I was already feeling a bit sensitive about the "weekend warrior" label. In actuality, I would put any of my fellow battery Marines up against any other Marines, active duty or not.

The PTT MP had gunny sign over some papers, and then the two prisoners were taken out of the truck, blindfolded and hands cuffed in back of them. That's right. Two fierce insurgents, one looking no more than 16 years old. All of this effort for two Iraqis.

We knew the two had been searched, but the manual said we had to search them again. LCpl Fowler gave me his M16, then he carefully searched them while the other seven of us stood at the ready, watching each and every move. They were clean, and we escorted them inside the wired compound. We sat them down and SSgt Cordero told us to remove their blindfolds.

Eyes blinking in the bright sunlight, they looked fearfully about. One guy was probably about 20 years old. He was a pretty big guy and had a few days stubble on his chin. There was a bruise forming along the side of his face. I wondered if he got that before or after his capture. He looked like he was trying to look tough, but I could see his fear. I could almost smell it.

The other insurgent was a skinny kid; he couldn't have weighed more than 130 lbs. He wasn't even trying to look tough—he was scared shitless. Justin Hansen stomped his foot at the kid, and he jumped about a mile.

"That's enough, Hansen," SSgt Cordero admonished him. "Check their zip ties and see if they're too tight or not."

"I was just messing with them," the lance corporal grumbled as he surrendered his weapon and checked the ties. With the kid, he just pushed him down on his side before giving the ties a yank. He tried that with the larger guy, but the Iraqi sat solidly and didn't let him push him all the way down.

The lieutenant came over to check on us, then later an interpreter came to join us. But mostly, we stood there in the hot sun, staring at the two Iraqis. The interpreter didn't even speak to them. I guess he was just there to listen in case either of the two started spilling out all the vital Al Qaeda super secrets.

As the largest of us, SSgt Cordero had me standing the closest to them. I think they were scared enough that the one inch I had over Hansen didn't make any difference.

Before I left for Iraq, I was watching a show on Discovery about this place in England where they rescued gorillas and chimps and monkeys. One little chimp had been abandoned, and the staff was trying to introduce it to the other chimps. The little guy was scared out of its wits. It wanted nothing to do with the other chimps. The young prisoner reminded me of that baby chimp. This guy was scared to his core. I'm sure he thought he was going to be killed. I'm pretty sure I would be scared, too, if Al Qaeda captured me, and he was just a kid.

On a hunch, I surrendered my weapon and got a bottle of water. As I approached the kid, he tried to scrunch back, but I merely held the bottle up, ready for him to drink. He hesitated, but finally opened his mouth, and drank, much of the water running down his face and onto his dirty T-shirt. I did the same with the other prisoner.

"Why you bothering with the ragheads?" Krispy Kreme asked.

"You know the regs. We have to provide them with adequate food, water, and shelter." After Abu Ghraib, the proper handling of prisoners was being stressed.

"Xenakis is right," SSgt Cordero said. "From now on, every 30 minutes, we give them water."

We stayed on duty for another four hours. A number of officers and staff made their way over to see the prisoners, but none stayed after satisfying their curiosity. For some of the fobbits, this was undoubtedly the first "enemy" they had seen. If they really were enemy, that is. The young guy didn't seem able to muster up the courage to fight anyone.

Eight new Marines came to relieve us. I was grateful to get out of the sun, and my stomach was growling for chow. As I left, I glanced back to see the kid staring at me. I wondered what was going on in his thoughts.

By the next morning, the two EPWs were gone, and I put them out of my mind.

# Chapter 4

*Camp Fallujah*
*April 5, 2006*

Nothing from Sig. I had waited almost 30 minutes to get a computer, and nothing. I had an e-mail from my mom and another from my little sister, but nothing from my wife. I had been in Iraq for over a month, I'd survived an IED, but I'd received only three e-mails from her.

I had called her several times. We had donated calling cards sent to us, so it wasn't too hard to get one and make the call. She hadn't answered most times I called, and the one time I reached her, she seemed distracted and said she had to go after only five minutes or so.

I had met Sig back in high school. We weren't from the same school, though. I was from La Quinta High, and she was from Westminster. We actually met one day at the food court at South Coast Plaza, and I think the idea of dating the "enemy" was alluring to both of us. She was a petite blonde from a well-off, devout Lutheran family. My family was more working class, and I was this big, swarthy Greek-American from an equally devout Orthodox family. I wasn't surprised that her family thought me beneath her.

Her family expected her to go to USC, but her grades weren't good enough, so she enrolled at Fullerton. I had a few scholarship offers for football, but I was done with school. I enlisted, and by the time I graduated boot camp and SOI, Sig had already dropped out of school. On a whim, we drove up to Vegas and got married.

Sig actually tried to be a good Marine Corps wife. Money was tight though, and before we really knew what it was like to live with each other, I was in Iraq. She took a job at WhatABurger and did the best she could while I had the adventure of my life. When I came back, she started to settle into married life, but then I went back to the war.

When my enlistment was over, I wanted to re-up, but she was having none of it. It was either her or the Corps. I told her I was required to serve out the remainder of my full enlistment as a reservist. I didn't tell her I could have done that in the IRR, the Individual Ready Reserve, where I would basically just keep the Marine Corps aware of how they could contact me. I found out that the SMCR battery, that is the drilling reserve battery, at Seal Beach was going to be deployed, and I joined it.

I guess I was less than honest with her. I was mad at her for how she was treating me now, but I also felt guilty for lying to her. I just hoped we could patch things up after I got back.

Brent Cooperage caught my eye as I left the computer shack. I shook my head. Brent was one of my closer friends here. He worked in the battery headquarters and had been stuck here at Camp Fallujah the entire time so far. He took out his frustrations in the gym, and as a gym buddy, you couldn't really ask for more. He was one of the few people who knew about my problems back at home.

"She'll come around. Just give her time," he said. He then tilted his head in the direction of the gym, them mimed doing a military press. "Ready to hit it?" he asked.

I smacked him on the shoulder. "I'm ready enough to lift you into the dirt!"

I was still feeling depressed, but lifting stacks of iron with Brent would go a long ways in sweating out some of my anxiety.

## Chapter 5

*Camp Fallujah*
*April 12, 2006*

"Stand by to stand by," SSgt Cordero muttered.

We'd been at the airfield for over an hour, waiting for the VIPs. From Fallujah, we were going to take them down to the government house in Ramadi for some meetings with the governor. Our VIP was the Director of USAID, a civilian, but I guess she was like a three-star general equivalent or something. She was going to travel with General Haskins, one of the two Marine one-stars at Fallujah. We'd escorted him before, and he was OK for a general.

It was brutally hot, and despite being here for going on two months, I wasn't completely used to the heat. I drank lots of water; good thing we had plenty of bottled water stashed in just about every nook and cranny aboard the camp.

I was just reaching for another bottle of water when two Hummers approached us from the buildings to the south of the airfield.

"OK, looks like game time," the staff sergeant said. "Let's get 'im ready."

The Hummer pulled up and the lieutenant hopped out first, followed almost immediately by the skipper. A more leisurely moment later, the general got out and stretched. He was a tall, well-built guy, but the helmet perched up on his head looked several sizes too small. You would think the Corps would have a helmet big enough for a general so that he didn't look like a Special Ed kid.

A couple of staff officers stepped out of the second Hummer but simply stood around it. They weren't going to come over here unless the birds were inbound, but it looked like we still had a few moments. The general's aide had already been with us waiting, and he hurried up to the general. That was one job I would never want.

I'd seen this lieutenant before, as well as the other aides, and they just seemed to be personal servants. I knew it was a good career move, but I'm glad corporals were not in the running for that job.

The general came up to SSgt Cordero and shook his hand, then reached up to LCpl Harris, the gunner on the gun vehicle, to shake his hand as well. It looked like he was going to make the circuit for all of us. General Haskins usually did this, but where for some O's it seemed fake, I felt that with him, he was sincere.

He was interrupted, though, when one of his staff pointed to the south. I looked up, and sure enough, two Black Hawks were making their way, coming up the east side of the camp to then pull a left to land at the airfield. As the general broke contact with us to get ready, Lieutenant Richmond came to attention as if to salute, old habits being what they were (we didn't salute here at Fallujah), but then simply nodded at the general before taking his place in the first gun vehicle. This was his preferred place in any convoy.

The Black Hawks landed, one after the other. I'm a Marine and all that, but I thought the Army Black Hawks were pretty mean-looking birds. I'd never been in one, but they looked like schoolyard bullies when compared to our Hueys. Before I left Iraq, I hoped I would get to ride in one.

The lead bird's crewchief hopped out first, tethered by his headset to the bird. He helped out someone in uniform, then someone short in civilian clothes, probably a woman, but it was hard to tell at this distance with the black vest and helmet she was wearing. On the second bird, however, there was no mistaking the long blonde hair flowing from under the helmet on the woman there.

"Damn!" Krispy Kreme muttered, and for once, I agreed with him.

All the passengers hurried to get out from under the rotors, then milled around a bit while the general strode forward to greet them. I could see him pointing back to us, and I thought we would load right up as per our convoy brief, but the short lady went into the plywood shack that acted as a terminal. It took me a moment to realize why. The heads in the back were a little crude, but full bladders have their own kind of power that brook no arguments.

The skipper and Gunny Pancoast were directing the rest of the passengers to our waiting Hummers. I was in a chase vehicle, so the plan was that I wasn't going to have any passengers with me, but people in the head shed do what they want, and Gunny brought up an Army major to me, telling me he would ride with us.

"Major Standuski, corporal," he said, shaking my hand.

"Corporal Xenakis," I replied. "Our driver is Corporal Meyers."

"Sir," Tony chirped, not getting out of the vehicle.

"Where do you want me?"

"Right here, sir," I told him, moving to hold open the right rear hatch.

We got in and waited for the rest of the convoy to load. The blonde girl walked past us to get into the Hummer in front of us. She looked even better up close, despite her black body armor. Both Tony and I must have been obvious, because there was a laugh in back of us from the major.

"Ah, yes, Brenda. She handles contracts for Al Anbar for USAID, and she is one of the benefits of working there. Not that I've noticed of course, being the married man that I am."

I turned to look back at the major, not knowing how to take that. He was a major, after all, and Army at that. He must have seen the expression on my face because he laughed again, and that brought out the laughs from both Tony and me. Who would've thunk it? A comedian major?

"If I wasn't so happily married, I might mention what she looks like on the stairstepper at the gym, especially if you're on one of the bikes in back of her, but as I am happily married, I won't do that."

Tony held out his fist for a bump, and I obliged. This major was OK.

The short woman finally came out of the terminal, and as the general was waiting for her, it was obvious to me that she was the VIP. She was escorted into the fourth Hummer, and at last, we were given the command to move out. The skipper and the gunny watched us leave. Both of them looked like they wanted to jump on board as well, but neither one of them got out of the camp very often, and that was mostly for meetings at the Fallujah government house. Like Brent, they must have been going a bit stir-crazy.

We made our way out of camp and started on the 40-minute ride to Ramadi. The dirt road and the paved highway to Ramadi were pretty open, but the closer we got to the city, the higher the pucker factor. Ramadi was a bigger city than Fallujah, and the fighting was more constant there. IEDs were a continual problem. The battery had not been hit there yet, knock on wood, but plenty of other Marines had. Army, too. There was an Army brigade taking half of the city, even if it was under Marine command.

Two days earlier, a grunt gunner on a Hummer had taken an RPG right in the chest while driving into the Al Anbar government compound. I never knew him, but I stepped into his memorial service at the Chapel of Hope to pay my respects. That easily could have been someone from the battery.

On my second trip into Ramadi, back in March, we'd taken some AK fire from a bozo near a small market. He was only about 20 yards away when he opened fire, but still he couldn't hit us. LCpl Dye was our gunner, and he started to swing about on the guy, but the lieutenant was with us on that trip, and he ordered Dye to hold his fire. The gunman had only fired off a burst before turning and running back into the market where other Iraqis were desperately diving for cover. The lieutenant made the right decision. A .50 cal opening up would have wrecked havoc, killing bystanders, and the gunman wasn't a threat anymore. What the incident impressed on me, though, was that anybody anywhere in this cesspit of a city could be targeting us. Anyone could take us as a target of opportunity.

As we entered the outskirts of the city, the radio chatter picked up a notch. Normally, we would first go to Camp Blue Diamond, but this time, it was straight to the government house. The roads got narrower, and all of us kept our eyes peeled for anything out of the ordinary: a dead goat, a bag of trash, a box—anything at the side of the road that could harbor an IED. We skirted several craters that had not yet been filled, reminders of what could happen.

I kept waiting for that something to happen, anything at all. It wasn't until I saw the walls of the government compound in front of us that I thought we were in scot-free. That thought must have pissed off the gods of the convoys because right then, the radios erupted. I hadn't heard any explosions or firing, but I could clearly hear Sgt Blount screaming to back up. He was the vehicle commander for the Hummer that was carrying the VIP. I tried to see around the Hummers in front of me, but while I saw two Hummers make the right turn into the compound, I couldn't see Blount's Hummer.

The Hummer in front of us shifted to the left, the gunner intent on what was in front. Then it became clear. Somehow, the shit-for-brains Craig had driven straight while every other vehicle was turning right into the compound. He was driving off into Indian country with the VIP inside.

Blount had him stopped, but there wasn't enough room for him to turn around.

"Tony, move forward on the right," I told my driver.

We didn't have a gunner, but with us up forward, abreast of the next Hummer, maybe we could be in position if the shit hit the fan. In front of us, a good 30 or 40 meters out there all alone, Blount's Hummer started backing up, weaving a bit from side to side. The radios were calling for updates, but we focused on any possible threat. After an eon, Craig finally was back far enough so he could put it back into forward and turn into the compound. He lurched it forward, then sped in, followed immediately by us. We turned into the compound just in time to see Craig take off the open door on one of the Hummers already inside and parked. We moved over further to the left and forward. In the now-doorless Hummer, General Haskins looked out. I don't know how to describe the look on his face, but it certainly wasn't good.

We pulled over and parked. I didn't know what to expect, but it certainly was not our VIP, all five feet of her, laughing when the general rushed up.

"Well, that was interesting. I'm not sure that would have been the meeting I was supposed to attend, but who knows what I could have accomplished out there?"

General Haskins started to apologize, but the woman waved him off.

"Shit happens, general. I'm sure you know that. Let's just get in to see the governor. I'll be glad to get out of all this armor."

By then Lieutenant Richmond was rushing up, but this time it was the general waving someone off, but with an I'll-take-this-up-with-you-later look on his face. The lieutenant skidded to a halt, then looked around for Krispy Kreme. Gunny Templeton and SSgt Cordero had beat him to it, though, with Cordero bodily pulling the idiot out of the driver's seat. I didn't really like the guy very much, but I winced as I considered his fate. I decided to steer as clear of all that as possible.

I got out of my Hummer and stretched. The area around the government house compound was more like what I imagined Fallujah would've looked like. The road in from Blue Diamond was not that bad, even if it was referred to as "IED Alley." But most of the buildings around the compound were down, either torn down or blasted down, I'm not sure. Inside the compound, the signs of violence were evident. Rubble was everywhere, and temporary patches could be seen all over the walls of the three buildings that made up the compound. Up against the side of the government house itself, there was even a black BMW, pretty mangled and looking much worse for wear.

"As I live and breathe, if it isn't Nick Xenakis! I thought you left our Big Green Machine!"

I turned around to see Derek Butler, one of my old K 3/4 Marines. "Sergeant" Butler, I should say, as I saw his new chevrons on his flak jacket.

"Well, damn, the Corps must be really scraping at the bottom of the barrel," I said, flicking at the chevrons with my forefinger as he came up. "Looks good there, though, you lifer."

We'd both been lance coolies and corporals together, and he was a hard-charger, someone you could count on. I still had a photo of him, Bob DeStafney, and me at the airport in Ireland on the way back from our first pump, beers in hand and raised in a toast.

"Ah, you know the Corps; they'll promote about anyone. Seriously, though, what're you doing here? I thought you were getting out and going home to make babies with your wife, Sig's her name, right?"

"I couldn't stay away, I guess. I joined the reserve battery out of Seal Beach, and now I'm back here as an MP."

"No shit? I don't know. If I got out, I think I'd stay out," he said. "Hey, let me give you the grand tour here. We rotate in and out of here to provide security."

I knew I wasn't going anywhere soon, so I figured why not? I told Tony I'd be back, then followed Derek between the main building and a smaller one to the side. Derek was giving me a rundown on his squad and how most of them were newbies when he ducked down and ran in a low crouch across a small open area. I followed suit.

"Oh yeah, I guess I should have mentioned that," he said as I ran up to where he'd stopped. "One building out there, at maybe 700 meters, gives the ragheads eyes inside, and every day or so, someone takes a shot. Those dipwads couldn't hit the side of a barn, but even a blind squirrel finds a nut every now and then."

We walked into a very rough building that seemed mostly made of plywood, at least from the inside. There were plywood partitions, plywood desks, plywood tables. Marines and civilians seemed busy as they went about their tasks.

"This is where we come in for a break. Civil Affairs is in here, pretty much for the duration, and some of the PRT is in here, too."

I really didn't know what a "PRT" was, but I figured by his gesture to two people that civilians were in it. He walked back to a small room, opened a refrigerator, and took out two Mountain Dews. I have to say, the cold soda felt pretty good going down.

There were some makeshift weights in the next room, or maybe the next partitioned area would be more accurate. An old guy was there lifting, but he was in Marine shorts and T-shirt, body armor on the floor beside him, so he must have been a Marine. I tilted my head at him in a question.

"That's a lieutenant colonel. He's worse than you. He already retired, but he volunteered to come back to this shithole. In six months, he'll probably never leave this compound."

As we walked back out, Derek poked his head into a small room. It was full of comm gear and one Marine. Normally, it would have been quite dark in there but for the hole in the overhead, only partially patched with a piece of plastic.

"A rocket came in last night, messed up some comm gear, but never even touched LCpl Evers here. Right, Evers?"

Evers, who had earphones on, merely lifted one hand, thumbs up, in reply.

"Seriously, though, I don't know how that guy made it. Not even a scratch," he told me as we left the building, ready to scrunch down and run back across the open area.

We went into the main building, and while the windows were all sandbagged, there was a semblance of normality inside. It was a pretty big building with high ceilings, and from what I could see, the offices looked like what you would expect pretty much anywhere.

We were walking down the main corridor when a door opened and a number of people came out. The general was there, along with our VIP. A swarthy-looking Iraqi with a scabbed and bruised face was leading them, and they were followed by a small, mousy-looking guy. After them were several colonels, MAJ Standuski, and Brenda, who looked even better out of her body armor. In back of them, I could see a servant picking up teacups in a rather ornate sitting room. They had spent all this time having tea?

"That's the governor," Derek told me, pointing out the guy with the beat-up face. "That other guy, he's the president of the Al Anbar council."

"He's the governor? So what happened to him? Cut himself shaving?"

"Did you see that Beemer outside?"

"Yeah, I saw it."

"He was driving it to work two weeks ago when a suicide bomber tried to get him again. Blew the shit out of himself and killed the governor's secretary and a bodyguard, but didn't get the gov. That makes 31 times they've tried to knock him off."

"Thirty-one times? Shit!" That BMW had been pretty much destroyed, and I wasn't sure how he'd managed to survive that.

"He just got that Beemer a week before. It was armored, so if it hadn't been, Al Anbar would be looking for a new governor." He paused for a moment before continuing, this time in a more subdued voice. "They did get his son a few months ago, though. Blew him up as he was coming here to the government house."

I watched the governor as he stopped by a big set of doors, motioning for our VIP to go inside. Since I'd been here, my mindset had been more of an us versus them, Americans versus Iraqis. But as he followed the Americans into the conference room, I realized that someday we would be leaving. The governor, if he managed to survive, would still be here. He had a lot more at stake than I had, than we had. In five months I'd be back at home watching the 'Niners on the tube, beer in hand, munching on chips and guac. The governor would still be trying to keep from getting blown up on his way to work.

I followed Derek as he climbed a set of wide, sweeping stairs. On the second floor, there were more offices, and Derek led me to a small door and up several sets of stairs until we came out into the sunshine on the roof. There were a number of Marines on the roof with comm gear, automatic weapons, grenade launchers, and M16s. Netting covered boxes and gear and provided just a bit of relief from the sun.

From this vantage point, Ramadi stretched out beneath us. All around the government compound the buildings were mostly rubble. Further out, they rose like abandoned buildings in some sort of end-of-the-world movie. Further still, they seemed more whole, more live, at least in comparison. For a city this size, there seemed very little life out there. There was very little of the hustle and bustle that living cities had.

Derek and I stood out of the way, under one of the nets. Seeing the Marines up there, I felt a pang of missing the grunts. This is what I was used to, not riding around in vehicles every day.

"Lieutenant, we've got another looker," a gunny said, coming up to the lieutenant who commanded the Marines on the roof.

"Where at? Show me." he said as he got up, binos in hand.

I had a pair of Bushnells with me that I had bought back before my second pump. They weren't issue, but they were handy to have around. When the gunny was pointing out to the lieutenant, I followed the directions and acquired the "looker" as well. On the roof of a building about 900 meters away, his head just peaking around some sort of wall on top of the roof, I could see him. He had his own glasses out and seemed to be observing us. The lieutenant watched him for a few moments as well.

"OK, get Cpl Lindt," he told the gunny, then lifted his own binos to take the Iraqi back under observation.

It was immediately obvious what Cpl Lindt's mission was. He was an odd-looking guy of average build, but his face was decidedly different and slightly out of whack. With half of a ghillie suit and his rifle, though, it was obvious that he was a scout-sniper. I'm not sure how much good a ghillie suit did on the roof of a building, but then again, I never went to sniper school. I respected the guys that did, though.

"We've got a looker over there, right on the roof of that building, about 90 mills to the left of the minaret," he said, holding three fingers up at arms length as he located the Iraqi. I want you to put a round beside him. Don't hit him, but let him know we'd rather not have him there."

"Aye, aye, sir," Cpl Lindt responded as he went to get his spotter. The two Marines went over to the side of the roof that faced the Iraqi and got into position. I kept watching, figuring that once the Iraqi saw the sniper get into position, he would boogie out of there. The spotter used the laser range-finder to get the distance (876 meters, I heard him say), then they started discussing windage and minutes. I had to listen again at that one. Minutes? I wasn't sure how minutes became sniper-targeting adjustments. Meanwhile, the Iraqi stayed put. Finally, Cpl Lindt settled in. From under his blouse, he pulled what looked to be a large sharp tooth on a chain, sticking the tooth between his teeth. He aimed downrange, took a breath, then let out a shot.

I was waiting for it, but I still jumped. I watched the building, and for a split second, thought the sniper had missed. I forgot about the distance, though, and how long it would take the round to travel that far. The stucco a foot or so alongside the Iraqi's head exploded. The Iraqi disappeared, and there were a few chuckles from the Marines on the roof. Cpl Lindt started to get back up when to everyone's surprise the Iraqi made a second appearance.

"Well, Cpl Lindt, I guess your message didn't get through. Give him another, this time closer," the lieutenant ordered.

The sniper shrugged, then got back into position. He already had his dope, so within only a few moments, a second round was on its way downrange. This time, the stucco only inches from the Iraqi's head exploded into dust. Once again, the man disappeared out of sight.

"That one's gotta hurt," the gunny said.

The stucco had to have peppered him, so I agreed with the gunny. Two shots, and he had to know he was being watched. So I was extremely surprised that he made another appearance, right in the same place. Was he a complete idiot? He had the glasses back up, and this time, it looked like he was on a cell phone or radio. Al Qaeda had blown up the main cell phone tower the week before, but it could have been a satellite phone. This was suddenly much more serious.

Several Marines called out to the lieutenant, but he had already seen the man for himself.

"Cpl Lindt, take him out now!"

What before had been slightly humorous was now all business. Cpl Lindt was already in position. I could see the Iraqi rise up a few inches as if to get a better look, phone or whatever still at his ear when the round went off. A long second or two later, it impacted full in the face of the Iraqi, a pink bloody mist blowing back from his head, and he collapsed in a heap. I could see his binos fall onto the rooftop and bounce a few feet away from his outstretched hand. Half of his body was in back of the small wall that he thought would protect him. The top half was out in the open, face up. We all watched to see if he was still alive, but we knew he had died instantly.

Cpl Lindt's spotter reached over and clapped him on the back. Lindt calmly backed up, then came away from the edge of the roof.

"Good job, Corporal," the lieutenant told him.

Lindt merely shrugged. I used to be a grunt, infantry. I've fired my weapon in combat, and I may have killed someone. I am not some bleeding bleeding-heart liberal afraid of doing my job. But Cpl Lindt's nonchalant attitude was a bit unnerving. I wasn't sure I would react the same. Thank God we had Marines like him on our side, though.

I glassed the figure on the far roof one more time. He hadn't moved. I thought I could see blood seeping out under him, but at this distance and angle, that it could have been my imagination.

I stayed on the roof with Derek for another ten 10 minutes or so before I told him I needed to get back down to be ready when our VIP was ready to leave. I knew she had a schedule to keep, and even though I knew I had more time, I felt like I should get back down to Tony and our Hummer.

I nodded at Cpl Lindt as I went over to the stairwell going down. He was munching on a Three Musketeers bar; he raised it to his forehead in a sort of salute in response as I left the roof.

## Chapter 6

*Camp Fallujah*
*May 16, 2006*

"Oh, sorry about that. I had to get a plumber for the sink, so that's why I took the money," Sig told me over the phone.

All my pay was going Direct Deposit, and of course, Sig had access to that. But we had agreed on a budget, and when I went to write a check for some cash, it bounced. I was called into the company office and given a lecture on fiscal responsibility from the first sergeant. I really didn't need too much cash, and the check had only been for $50, but Sig couldn't even leave that amount in the account for me.

At least we were talking. This was three weeks in a row that we had connected. I wanted that to continue, so I held down what I really wanted to say.

"OK, Sig. I understand. But please try and keep at least $100 in the account. And if you can't, send me an e-mail. We're getting charged $35 for a bounced check now."

"OK, folks, wrap it up. We're going into blackout," the civilian who managed the phone center called out.

I felt the familiar lump in my throat. We went into blackout on the phones and on the internet when someone was killed. Some Army wives had been told via e-mails about their husbands being killed before the chaplain and officers could tell them in person, so now, all over Iraq, we were cut off until the next of kin were notified.

"OK, Sig, I gotta go. The phone's are getting cut off. I'll call you again on the weekend."

I hung up, then looked around. No use trying to get online; those would be cut off, too. I still had three hours before I had duty. Hitting the gym seemed as good a bet as anything else. I didn't know if Brent was on or not, so I wandered over to the company office.

"You free?" I asked him as I entered the office.

"Nah, not for awhile. You going to the gym?"

"Yeah, I'm on at 1200."

"Better hit it without me." I turned to go when he added, "Hey, didn't you tell me you knew a sergeant at Ramadi . . . Butler?"

I felt my heart drop. I simply nodded.

Brent reached over and looked through some papers. "Derek Butler?"

I nodded again.

"Man, he was killed this morning. A sniper got him at the government house. He's already on the casualty report."

"A sniper?" I asked stupidly. "But he told me the Iraqis can't shoot like that. They just 'inshallah' it and hope for the best."

I felt cheated. He told me the Iraqis couldn't shoot. So how could he have been killed? It was like he broke some sort of contract, and irrationally, I felt he lied and was at fault. I knew this was irrational, but I couldn't help the feeling.

"Could have been a Chechen," Brent said.

"Chechen?"

"Yeah, like from Russia. Haven't you read any of the intel? Some of the Russian ragheads are over here training our ragheads, and they were all trained as Soviet snipers. They might be Muslims, but they don't hold to that 'inshallah' crap. They're supposed to be pretty good."

I knew the Russians were fighting in Chechnya. I just hadn't realized that their rebels were down here. It didn't really matter anyhow. Derek was dead.

## Chapter 7

*The Green Zone*
*July 1, 2006*

"As usual, plans have changed," the colonel said as he came up to us.

Me and Tony had been assigned to this colonel, another reservist working in the Green Zone. He had flown up to Fallujah for a meeting, and this was the result of that meeting. He had flown back, but me and Tony were assigned a cargo Hummer and joined a convoy to the Green Zone. We were going to take school supplies back to Fallujah to give to the Iraqis.

The colonel had met us as we came in, then told us to wait. So we waited. And waited. At least there was a semblance of shade, with all the trees surrounding the parking lot outside the embassy. About three hours later, the colonel came back out.

"The convoy from Kuwait with the supplies is still at Al Asad. It won't come in until late tonight or early tomorrow morning. So you're going to overnight it here."

"What about the convoy back, sir? We're scheduled at 2300," I asked.

"No problem. I've already contacted your command, and you're now on a convoy for tomorrow night. I'll get you the points of contact a little later. Now, the question is: What do we do with you two? Do you have locks for your weapons?"

"No, sir," we answered in unison.

Normally, we carried flexible cable locks, but this wasn't our normal Hummer, and both of us had forgotten to transfer them to this vehicle.

"Well, that makes it more difficult. I'll put it up to you, then. I've got one extra lock you can borrow. But you can spend today, tonight, and tomorrow here in the vehicle, or you can go buy an extra lock at the PX, and we'll get you a rack for the night."

"We'll buy one, sir," I answered immediately.

"Yeah, I thought as much," he said with a smile on his face. "Let me take you to billeting, and you can ask them there about where to park your vehicle for the night. We'll get you a temporary pass for the embassy so you can help with the supplies tomorrow, and then you're on your own until say, 1000 tomorrow, right here? Think you can handle that?"

"Yes, sir," we almost shouted, again in perfect unison. A whole day and night off? In the Green Zone? We could handle that.

"OK, let's get you billeted first. Leave your Hummer here for now and follow me."

I never had an O6 guide before. Maybe there were so many colonels up here at the big head shed that this was normal duty for them. It was different at Fallujah. The regimental commander was a colonel, too, just like this guy. He'd taken a rocket in the arm on the first day of his last pump and almost bought it, but now he was back again for a second shot at command. Somehow, I couldn't picture him playing guide to two corporals. This colonel, though, was happily pointing out the sights as we walked between the tall walls of the embassy and some smaller buildings and what looked like hundreds of trailers.

We turned in at a large pool. It was around lunchtime, and there were a number of people, both in uniform and civvies lounging around, eating and drinking. Some of the civilians were quite openly drinking beer. I wasn't a huge drinker, but the sight got my attention.

Two women in bikinis got my attention as well. There were armed soldiers, airmen, and a few Marines and sailors, and there, not five or six feet from them, two women in bikinis were walking by. It was surreal.

The colonel led us into a trailer where he told a civilian that we needed two racks for the night. The civilian, an older guy with a deep Southern accent, tried to say they were pretty full at the moment, but the colonel was having none of that. He insisted, and lo and behold, racks were found. I guess having eagles on your collar does have some advantages.

We were given bedding, two keys, and a map. We found out where to park our Hummer and where to get our passes. The colonel gave us his phone number in case there were any problems and then left. We followed the map through what had to be hundreds of white trailers. If they didn't all look exactly the same, we could have been in any trailer park back home. With only one wrong turn that took us a bit of time to figure out, we finally found our trailer. There were a few wooden steps leading up into it. The trailer was split into separate apartments. We went into the far-left one. There were two racks, a small desk, and a chair. The racks would also act as rifle racks after we locked our weapons to them.

We dumped the bedding, then locked up and went to move the Hummer and get our passes. First stop would be the PX, but we wanted time to explore a bit after that. Moving the Hummer took only minutes. Getting our passes took longer, but the colonel had already greased the skids, so it wasn't too bad. We were pretty hungry by then, so it was off to chow. The DFAC was bigger than ours at Fallujah, but it was pretty much the same as far as chow went. Two lines served up the main courses, then there was the salad and fruit bar, some other dishes, and the dessert line. Tony wanted burgers, so he went into another section off to the left for the burger line. The ranks were a little higher here than in Fallujah, and there were more civilians, but chow was chow.

We didn't hurry, but we didn't waste time, either. I did get some ice cream, though. I don't know if it was Coldstone quality, but I have to admit I sure liked it. Without beer in Iraq, ice cream was my biggest vice.

After chow, we walked over to the PX. It was a little small, but it had a good selection. Tony bought the lock (he didn't have a wife emptying his account). Outside the front doors, there were some Iraqi vendors. I wanted to buy some old Iraqi money one guy was selling, but I decided against it. There was a Subway though, and the smell of fresh bread almost drew me in even if I had just eaten. There was even a car dealer. You could buy your car in Baghdad, then pick it up when you got back home.

I was surprised by the number of foreign uniforms. I knew the Brits were in the fight pretty heavily, and there were Poles and

Spaniards and Australians fighting, but I saw people with patches from Georgia, El Salvador, New Zealand, Azerbaijan, Latvia, Fiji, Mongolia, Honduras, and probably more that I didn't catch. I'm not sure if they really represented fighting forces or if they were just there to show their countries' support for the Coalition of the Willing.

Camp Fallujah was a huge improvement over my first two tours, but the Green Zone had Fallujah beat to hell. We could almost be back in the US. Almost, but not quite. We didn't have to wear body armor and walk around armed back in Cali.

"Hey, what d'ya say about that pool back there? You up for it?" Tony asked me.

Nicer than Fallujah or not, the weather here was the same, and the thought of that big pool was inviting.

"Sounds good to me," I replied.

We went back to our hootch. Both of us had brought our assault packs with us. They couldn't carry a lot, but when we were on a convoy, it always made sense to have a few necessities, and shorts and shower shoes were par for the course. We changed into the shorts, kept our T-shirts on, then walked over the big pool just outside the embassy. There were a lot of people there, even early in the afternoon when you'd figure they'd be at work, but we found a table under a big tree where we could ground our gear.

"Now don't you get burned, there," Tony said with a laugh as I took off my shirt. "You're looking awfully white."

I looked down at my chest, and yeah, I was pretty white. I wasn't sure if I'd had my shirt off in the sun since we arrived. I hadn't planned on beach ops, so I didn't have sunscreen. I could smell sunscreen though, so some of the others at the pool must have some.

Tony saw me looking around. "That's it. You just go up to one of those delectable young ladies and ask them to lay some on you, rub it in good. Hell, I might try that line myself."

"Yeah, right."

"I'm serious, dude. A brother can burn, too. Just not as fast as you white boys."

I just rolled my eyes. I was just going to have to watch my exposure. I walked to the edge of the pool, feeling the sun burning into my shoulders. Without hesitating, I dove in. After so many months here in this dustbowl of a country, the feeling of the cool water surrounding me was heaven. I sunk to the bottom of the pool and just lay there until the need for oxygen brought me back up. I could almost feel layers and layers of dust, grit, and sand just roll off me.

I stood there a moment, just relishing the feeling until I had to jump out of the way. About half of the pool was being used by lap swimmers, so I moved over to the edge where I wouldn't be in the way. Tony dove in, but instead of joining me, he started doing laps.

I passed my swimming tests OK, but I wasn't a great swimmer. I knew I could use the workout, but I wasn't in the mood. I just wanted to relax for awhile, forgetting Iraq, forgetting convoys, forgetting Fallujah. I just watched the swimmers go back and forth, my mind wandering. Finally, I notice the first twinge of burn on my shoulders. I ducked down, got wet, then got out of the pool, going back to our table, but not before grabbing a cold bottle of water.

I sat there sipping the water, for once not having anything to do. Tony kept plugging away at the laps. It was a bit mesmerizing just watching him. I finished the water, then looked around. I was under a huge tree, really immense. California had its redwoods and sequoias, and this one was not nearly so tall, but it spread over a huge amount of ground. Hanging from one branch was a swing of some sort. Curious, I got up and walked over to it. It was a pretty simple thing, just a seat suspended by a rope. I reached out and gave it a push."

"That's Uday's swing," a voice called out.

I looked over to see two soldiers lounging at another table.

"Pardon me?"

"Uday. Saddam's son. That's his sex swing."

"Really?" I said as I stepped back to look at it.

"Yepper. He used to find girls walking on the street or at parties, then bring them back here and fuck them on that swing. He even killed one officer who wouldn't let him dance with his wife, then brought the widow back right there and fucked her."

I'd heard lots of stories about Uday, about how he raped people, how he murdered people, how he tortured athletes who didn't perform well, but I didn't know how much of that was true. I looked back at the swing. The soldier could be pulling my leg, or he could be just repeating an urban legend. I mean, how practical was a swing for rape? But just the possibility that Uday Hussein had raped girls right there brought a shudder to me. I involuntarily stepped back, as if to distance myself from it. I shook my head and turned to go back to our table.

"Yeah, pretty fucked up, there. At least the bastard got what he deserved, courtesy of the 101st," the soldier said, as he lifted up his fist for a bump from his buddy.

I sat back down and looked back into the pool. Tony was still going at it, swimming strongly. I figured he had to stop soon, but it was at least another 45 minutes until he quit. He pulled himself out of the water and came over to the table, barely breathing hard.

"What are you, some sort of freaking fish?"

"What, you think a brother can't swim, right? You forget I'm a SoCal boy, born with a surfboard under my feet. I can outswim anyone in the battery, dude," he said, drawing out the "dude" into almost a surferboy parody.

I realized that me and Tony had been riding together for a couple of months now, but I didn't know much about his private life, who he was. I'd pretty much assumed he was from Compton or East LA, but now I felt a little guilty for that. Now that I thought of it, there really was more of a beach and surfer tone than 'hood to his voice.

It still struck me a bit odd that two corporals were assigned together to a vehicle, but that was the reserves for you. Ranks did different jobs than they might do in the active forces. If this were an active duty unit, I would expect a PFC or lance coolie to be the drivers, not corporals.

We hung out at the pool for another hour or so, chatting about nothing much, at least not Marine Corps. I found out that Tony's father was some sort of big-time aeronautical engineer, that they lived down in San Luis Obispo in a big house overlooking the Pacific. Tony had been a water polo star in school and had enrolled at UC Davis with a scholarship. He joined the reserves after 9/11 while still an undergraduate and stayed in to make this deployment even if that interrupted his grad school plans. I asked him if he had a degree, why wasn't he an officer. He said he just liked firing the big guns, and officers didn't get to do that.

I told him about my life: my family, my high school, playing ball, even my problems with Sig. I hadn't planned on it, but I felt I really got to know Tony better. I was just sorry it had taken four months to do it.

Eventually we got up and went back to our hootch. The heads were communal at the end of each line of trailers, so we showered and cleaned up before chow. We had showers at Fallujah, of course, but somehow, I felt cleaner than I had felt since landing in Kuwait.

Chow was great, as usual. There wasn't much in the way of salad, though, and I was surprised to hear people bitch about it. A sign on the front hatch informed us that the convoy bringing fresh vegetables had been hit, so why the bitching? That is what the war boiled down to for them? That Shia insurgents kept them from eating fresh salad?

After chow, we wandered over to the gym. I didn't have my gear, but I wanted to check it out. There had to have been 200 people there, all on a huge number of bikes, stair steppers, treadmills, whatever. The equipment would have put any commercial gym back in Orange County to shame.

As we were leaving, we noticed a crowd of people gathering outside. We wandered over, and to my surprise, they were about to begin a dodgeball tournament, just like in that Ben Stiller movie. The teams had crazy names, and the atmosphere was pretty festive. It wasn't like we had anything better to do, so me and Tony climbed up the wall around the court and sat down to watch. The announcer—who looked like he might be Air Force, given his blue shorts—was pretty funny, giving commentary as the teams went into battle. I think most of the players must have been civilian, and most had dressed in a pretty crazy fashion with mismatched socks, outrageous shirts, and what have you. At least a third were women. One short, heavyset woman must have been some sort of ringer. She was deadly with the ball, knocking off big, buff-looking guys with ease. Her team won their first round, but on the second, the entire opposing team took her out with a concentrated volley.

As the championship match started, I heard automatic firing off behind us. From the wall, we could see over the river and into Baghdad. The firing picked up, and explosions joined the chorus. Two Apache helos showed up, pouring fire into the buildings below. Over there, not 1,000 meters away, people were in a life-and-death struggle. People were fighting, killing, dying. Meanwhile, 10 feet below me, Americans, Brits, and others were dressed in funny clothes playing a kids' game as if everything was fine in the world.

## Chapter 8

*The Green Zone*
*July 2, 2006*


I couldn't help but to gawk as I carried a box of supplies. The embassy was pretty amazing, like some sort of palace out of *1001 Nights*. There was marble everywhere. I had thought Ramadi's government house was pretty impressive, but this place had it dead to rights. In one rotunda, there were cameras set up and lights ready for some sort of statement. I could see CNN, FOX, BBC, and a host of other signs on the cameras. We nonchalantly walked through them and out the front door.

Me and Tony weren't the only ones acting like coolies. The colonel and a major were carrying boxes just like us. We had taken two trips so far, and between the four of us, we had another two trips or so after this in order to get the school supplies loaded.

Plans had changed since yesterday. There wasn't a convoy going to Fallujah tonight, so we were joining one to Al Asad, then we'd make the trip to Fallujah tomorrow morning. Tonight would be with the big rigs with the Army in charge. I wasn't sure yet about tomorrow.

It was quite a long way from the major's office up on the second floor all the way out past security and to the Hummer out in the parking lot. The five trips took us well over an hour. I was surprised that the colonel and the major stuck it out and helped. It wasn't as if me and Tony had anything better to do, and they were both O's, after all. High O's, at that.

After the last load, we went back into the embassy. We'd have to have one of us on the vehicle until we left, but the colonel said it would be OK for the moment, what with the guards not 20 meters away. We went back inside where the colonel handed us an inventory sheet. I thought we would have to go out and count each item and then sign the sheet, but he just handed it to us and seemed to forget it. He told us he would fly in on the 5th and that he would contact command to see about delivery. I got the feeling that this was supposed to get media coverage, so there would probably be more people involved than just the three of us.

On the way back to the Hummer, while still in the embassy, Tony pulled me aside. "Look at that! They've got paninis here!" he exclaimed, excitement in his voice.

I knew that was some sort of sandwich, but I'd ever had one. We had eaten chow before taking out the boxes, but food was food, and seasoned Marines knew to eat whenever the opportunity arose. There was a sign-in sheet, and I wondered if anyone was going to count signatures to see if we were eating too much, and even if I knew that was a little paranoid, I messed up my signature a bit to make it hard to read.

This little cafeteria was seemingly just thrown into an available space. On one side of the main passage, they had a small selection of dishes. I picked my bread, then loaded up on the sliced meats, especially the roast beef. I stuck on some mayo, then had to decide between no less than five types of mustard. I ended up putting one on one half, then another on the other half. We walked across the passage, dodging people hurrying back and forth, then to another area where tables were set up. There were four rather large machines there. I watched Tony lift up the top half of the machine, then put his sandwich on the hot plate before closing the lid back down. I reluctantly followed suit. This was going to smash my sandwich.

After about two minutes, Tony opened his press up and took his sandwich out. Again, I copied him, took out my sandwich, and followed him to a seat. My sandwich was pretty flat with large grill marks running across the bread. Food was food, though, so I took a bite . . . and was pretty impressed. This was good!

"Do you hear that?" Tony asked me quietly.

"What?" I asked, my mouth full of sandwich.

"Just listen. That table in back of us. That guy talking, he just said he's gay."

I turned around, hopefully not too obviously. There were eight people at the table, mostly civilians. There were two soldiers, but with their backs to me, I couldn't see their ranks. They were older, though, so they were probably up there. Three were what looked like American women, one looking surprisingly young. One pretty fat guy with a beard sat there in rapt attention. The final two were probably Iraqis, an older woman and the guy Tony said was gay.

Gay or straight, I didn't care much one way or the other. Don't ask, don't tell seemed to work for me. But now with Tony pointing him out, I was drawn in to listen.

". . . couldn't figure out who they were, so I had to guess which ID card to use."

Even I could see the fat guy pull back in puzzlement.

"You don't know, George?" the Iraqi guy asked. "Well, most of us now carry two ID cards. A card will tell others immediately if you are Sunni or Shia. So we carry two. If we're stopped by Sunnis, we show the one that makes us look like a Sunni. If we're stopped by Shia, we use the other one."

I hadn't heard that, but it made its own kind of sense.

"Unfortunately for me, I chose the wrong one. I was pulled out of the bus along with 10 other men."

I couldn't imagine being grabbed like that, being held by gunmen. I think I'd fight to the death before I allowed that to happen to me.

"They lined us up kneeling on the side of the road. We had our hand over our heads. I knew it was bad, and I tried to make my peace with Allah. I knew what would happen. All I could think of was that my family might never know, that they might never find my body."

All of the people were spellbound. Even I was, sitting at the next table. The man's English was fluent, if accented, but I barely noticed that.

"The leader gave his speech, then they went to the first man. They pulled his hands down and in back of him, then pulled his shirt down halfway to act as handcuffs," he said, using his hands to mimic the motion. "Then one of the gunmen shot him in the head."

Two of the women gasped, hands covering their mouths.

"They went to the next man, or boy, really. He couldn't have been much more than 14. He was killed in the same way. They kept moving down the line. You have to imagine it. The voices praying, pleading for mercy. The loud report of the gun, the thud of the falling body. The smell of gunpowder. I tried to blank it all out. I was sixth in line. The fifth man fell against me when they shot him. I could feel his blood as it splattered me. I felt arms pulling my hands down, then my shirt was yanked down. I waited for the end, but it didn't come. I told you that gays are considered against Allah, against the Qur'an. Fundamentalists think we should be executed. So we're not open about our lives. That is why the one thing we do is shave our chests, our one way of saying who we are, but where no one else can normally see it.

"Well, they saw my chest, then they started shouting that I was Satan's spawn, I was evil and damned to hell. Someone hit me with a rifle stock, and I fell. I kept waiting for the bullet to end it when they started shouting I should be punished. So for my punishment, they raped me. All eight of them took turns, raping me, yelling at me while they did it that I'm going to hell.

"When they were done, the left me there, bloody and lying in the dust. Like nothing happened, they went to the next man and killed him, and they killed all the rest."

I was in disbelief while he talked. It didn't make sense. But I could see the man, hear the truth in this voice.

"I laid there for at least 30 minutes, unable to move. I don't know if that was shock or if I was just afraid if I moved, they'd come back and kill me. I know people saw us, but no one came forward. Finally, I got up and left, ignoring the dead men, just grateful to be alive."

There was silence at the table for a moment. The Iraqi woman reached over to put a hand on one of the man's, then looked at one of the soldiers.

"That's why we need your help, colonel. We've talked about women's rights, about gay rights, but unless we get you Americans to pressure the new government, nothing will happen," she said.

As their conversation got into politics, I turned back to look at Tony.

"That's messed up," he simply said.

That was an understatement. I just couldn't get my mind around what I had heard. They thought he was Satan because he was gay, then "punished" him by raping him? It just didn't make sense. What did that make them? I began to wonder just how we could bring peace to Iraq if we were so fundamentally different. I didn't mean what they thought about gays. Some Americans think that is a sin, too. But their punishment? How could a supposedly straight man physically perform that? And if being gay was such a sin, they let him live and finished killing the rest of the guys?

This country was certifiable crazy, la-la land.

It wasn't just this country. The Green Zone itself was surreal. In Fallujah, we were a combat camp. It made sense. I understood it. Here, it was a different story.

I looked around at the other tables at people with laptops, in earnest conversations, sipping their Green Bean coffee or munching on paninis. Take off the uniforms, get rid of the weapons, and we could be back in Anytown, USA. Just like the night before at the volleyball tournament, I felt the disconnect. We were in Oz, far removed from the war. I wonder how many people here, the ones calling the shots, even knew what we went through out there in the field, out there in the sand, the heat, and most of all, the fighting.

I took another bite of my sandwich. I was in Oz at the moment, our own version of the Emerald City. Soon enough, though, I would be expelled and back out in the real world, or at least, what was our real world. I just hoped that whoever the wizard was here, he had some sort of plan and we were not out there fighting flying monkeys and evil witches on our own.

# Chapter 9

*Outside of Fallujah*
*July 3, 2006*

"Almost there," I muttered, reaching over to punch Tony in the shoulder, waking him. Technically, he shouldn't have been asleep, but we'd been up for almost 30 hours and counting.

The convoy to Al Asad had been a goat rope. Well, maybe that wasn't accurate. The Army had it pretty well organized. But we had waited and waited in the staging area. The big semis just couldn't seem to get ready. I had been pretty frustrated as the hours crept by.

I didn't envy the truck drivers, despite their good pay. They took their rigs from Kuwait to all over Iraq. Sometimes they had Americans providing security, sometimes not. Sometimes, security was even from Iraqi forces. It was a dangerous job, and more than a few drivers had been killed. Still, I wanted to get out and start kicking some ass to get the show on the road.

Finally, we pulled out, and even with one stop out there in the middle of nowhere, we made it to the base. There, we had to try and hook up with our ride back to Fallujah. No one seemed to know where we could make contact, and by the time we did, it was already light. We had breakfast in the DFAC, then stood by the Hummer and waited. Tony looked pretty beat, so I told him I'd take over.

Tony liked to joke that I was his A-driver. Actually, I was the vehicle commander, but for this leg, I guess I was the A-driver. We pulled out around 0830, and after about 30 minutes, Tony started to drift off. We were in a convoy with plenty of security, so I just let him catch some z's.

We were not going directly into camp first. We were going into the government compound. From there, some of us would then break off and return to base. Then it would be time for a shower and hitting the rack for a couple of hours, at least.

Tony yawned, then wiped some drool that had dried on his chin. "You OK?" he asked.

"Yeah, no problem. We'll be pulling in in a couple of minutes."

I was always a little hyped when we were driving around, especially in a built-up area. I'd been hit twice already, even if one of those times, that gunman in Ramadi, wasn't much of an incident, but I hoped the Gods of Ambushes thought that was enough for one tour. With our destination almost in sight, though, I could begin to relax. Just another 500 meters, turn right, and the last 200, and we'd be home free.

"You know, I've been meaning to ask you, what . . ."

I never did hear what Tony was going to ask as a huge explosion rocked the Hummer and threw us to the left. All I could see was flames as we spun around several times before slamming to a halt up against a wall.

*Good Lord, not again!*

The Hummer was flooded with light. I turned around, and most of the back of the vehicle was mangled and gone. Something had blown right through us, shearing a huge portion of the Hummer away.

The sounds of gunfire began to register, even if, like the first time I was hit back in February, my ears were ringing something fierce. More than a few rounds hit us, one striking the back of my seat an inch from me.

"Let's go, let's go!" I shouted at Tony. We had to get out of the line of fire.

The Hummer had spun around so that the front was now pointed back towards the way we came, but canted a bit so that there was room between the passenger door and the wall of the building so that Tony had room to get out. I was now on the street side of the road, open to incoming fire. I grabbed my M16 and rolled out, landing hard. I scrambled up and started sprinting to one of our gun Hummers, anxious to get under its protection. I reached it and looked back for Tony. I would have sworn that he was right behind me, but as I looked, I could see he hadn't moved from his seat. He was still there, and I could see rounds impacting on what was left of the wreck.

Above me, the .50 cal was opening up, responding to the incoming fire. I was about to ask the driver to take me back to my Hummer, but the crew was heavily engaged. I knew this was on me.

I slung my M16, took a deep breath, and ran back to the Hummer, diving behind it where it gave me at least a bit of cover. I reached up for Tony and blanched. I felt my gorge rise. Whatever hit us had taken out part of his seat, and with it, a good portion of his back. His flak jacket was a mangled mess, and part of his right shoulder was simply gone.

I grabbed the left side of his harness, which was still intact, then pulled him up and over the gearbox, out of the driver's door, and to the ground.

"Tony, you OK, bud? You with me?" I asked, searching his face for any signs of life.

He was breathing, but labored and with a raspy sound to it. This wasn't good. I'd have to carry him back to the other Hummer.

More rounds started impacting around us. I peeked around the wreck. Up on the roofs opposite us, I could see shadowing figures popping up, drawing the fire from our vehicles. This was a pretty big ambush. We were close to the government compound, so a reaction force would get here soon. The ambushers would melt away then, but they wanted to do as much damage as they could in the meantime. I just had to keep Tony alive for a few more minutes.

More by instinct than by conscious thought, I raised my M16 and fired off a few rounds at the rooftop opposite us. I doubt if I hit anyone, but I thought it might help keep their heads down. I ducked back down behind the hulk when a burning lance of fire went shooting through my right leg. I fell back, grabbing it. Blood pooled out between my fingers. A round had come under the wreck and hit my shin just below my knee and exited my calf. I thought shock was supposed to deaden the pain, but this hurt like a mother fucker!

Another round came zipping under, but missing us. I don't know if they were purposely aiming that way, or if these were stray rounds. I didn't think the Iraqis on the roofs had the angle to get the rounds that low. When a third round came in and hit the front tire, I knew I had to get Tony out of there. I looked around. I wasn't sure how my leg would hold up carrying him to the gun Hummer. Just to my right, though, whatever had taken out the back of my Hummer had put a hole in the wall, not five meters away. It was plenty big enough for me to drag him in and out of the line of fire.

Although his flak jacket was mangled, the harness I used to pull him out of the Hummer still looked secure on his left side, so I took ahold of it and got ready. I almost fell as I stood up, but I knew I just had to gut it out. Normally, I could lift him with ease, but now I knew I was going to have to drag him.

I took a deep breath, then tried to run, pulling Tony behind me. It was more of a lurch instead of a run, but it would only take me a few moments to get him there. I was halfway when I was slammed in the back and knocked down. I knew I had taken another round, but I didn't have time to check if my flak jacket had stopped it or not. I got back up and pulled Tony another step, then two more. One more step, and we were inside, into the darkness and safety.

I started to look around to get my bearings. I only briefly caught the AK butt coming at my face before it smashed into me and all went dark.

# Chapter 10

*Fallujah*
*July 3, 2006*

As my eyes focused, I saw concrete swaying. It took me a moment to realize that I was being carried, face down. The concrete wasn't swaying—I was. Someone had my arms and legs, and I was being bodily carried face down through a narrow hallway as harsh, guttural Arabic surrounded me. As soon as the realization hit me, the pain hit me as well. My leg was on fire, and someone was gripping it tightly.

We came to a doorway or something and hesitated; sunlight lit the floor a foot beneath my nose. A drop of crimson splattered, making a flower on the dusty concrete floor. Despite the pain, I was momentarily fascinated by it, that splash of color in a world of grey. Only peripherally did I realize I was bleeding from my face.

There was more shouting. I don't speak Arabic, but even in my muddled, pain-filled consciousness, I could tell that they were arguing. I could hear panic in some of their voices. Someone evidently won the argument, because we rushed out the door. The men carrying me were not in unison, and each step brought jolts of pain to my battered body.

"Where's Tony?" I asked, trying to twist my body to look back.

No one answered or made any indication that they had heard me. I tried to look ahead to see if he was being carried as well, but with the running and jerking, I couldn't really hold my head up. I just hoped he was still alive.

We jerked to a stop, and the guy holding my right leg kept going forward to get up against the wall, nearly tearing it off in the process. I screamed in agony. In response, someone hit me upside the head. Even dazed as I was, I got the message to keep quiet, but wanting to keep quiet and keeping quiet when your leg was being ripped off were two different things.

I wasn't really scared at the time. I should have been. I was hurt and being carried out of the battle, away from my fellow Marines, by insurgents. We'd all seen the videos of what Al Qaeda in Iraq and Shia insurgents did to their prisoners. But in the fog that muddled my brain, broken by the lances of pain that wracked my body, and my concern for Tony, I think fear was crowded out. There just wasn't room for it.

I was carried into another building just as the whup-whup of a helo flew overhead. For a moment, I thought maybe my rescue had arrived. The men holding me froze, as if the helo's crew could hear them if they spoke. When the sounds of the helo faded, they started moving again. I was taken to a corner and unceremoniously dropped.

I screamed again, but this time I was ignored. Face planted on the concrete floor, I could smell my blood as it pooled around my cheek and mouth. The metallic tang that I smelled was the last sense I retained as I fell back into unconsciousness.

# Chapter 11

*????*
*July 3? July 4?*

I slowly came to. I was lying on the floor, my hands behind me. I couldn't see anything but a diffused light. I realized I had a hood over my head. I tried to bring my arms around in front of me, but they were tied together at the wrist. The effort drew some pain from my back, but it wasn't too bad. My leg, though, ached something fierce, and my nose was swollen, making breathing difficult, especially with the hood over my head.

I could hear the sounds of talking going on but none of the sounds of battle. Either the fight was long over or I was pretty far removed from it. I was thirsty, but I had no idea how long I had been out. My left arm was numb from being underneath me, so I tried to shift a bit to take the pressure off.

I must have made a sound because the talking around me ceased. Footsteps approached me, then the hood was ripped off my head, tearing the scabs where it had gotten stuck in the congealed blood on my nose, bringing a new burst of pain and starting the bleeding once again. I blinked in the light and looked up at a rather large Iraqi. At least I assumed he was Iraqi. I knew there were foreigners fighting here. Al Qaeda in Iraq was mostly foreigners, and while we didn't face them much in Al Anbar, Iranians were supposedly fighting for the Shia. But I sure couldn't tell a foreigner from an Iraqi. All I knew was this guy looked like trouble.

He gave me a light kick on the side, more of a nudge, then turned back to the others, saying something that got them to laugh. He knelt then, putting his AK on the deck, staring at me. He didn't look like he was angry. His face was a blank.

With his left hand, he grabbed the front of my utility blouse and hauled me up about a foot or so, so my face was closer to his. I stared back at him, trying not to show fear. Without warning, he brought his right hand around in a roundhouse slap, knocking me across the face. My nose exploded again, and the shock nearly put me back down. The pain was incredible, and the blood, which had been flowing again, became a gush that ran into my mouth. I started choking, unable to breathe through my nose and now having my throat full of blood.

Despite this, despite my panic to draw in air, I couldn't help but notice his face filling my vision. He still looked calm and detached. It was like he didn't even hold me in enough regard to be concerned. Slowly, he reached up and placed his hand over my mouth, cutting off my air.

In high school, I was taught about Maslow and his hierarchy of needs. We had had discussed it in class, and at the time, it seemed too simplistic to me. Just another academic dance to justify the academic lifestyle. But when you can't breathe, all else fades away into being inconsequential. I didn't care that I was thirsty, that I hurt all over, that I was a prisoner, that I wanted to put on a brave face to them. I just wanted to breathe. I had to breathe. I started to struggle, to push against him the best I could with my hands and feet tied.

He was a big strong guy, but I was fairly big myself, and I had the added motivation of trying to get air. I twisted away from him, then twisted back as hard and as fast as I could. I managed to get my mouth past his hand and took a gulp of air, but I got blood down my windpipe and started to choke and cough. He pulled me back up and stared at me again while I coughed and tried to get in some air.

I think someone must have said something to him because he looked back over his shoulder and shrugged before letting go. I fell back, bouncing my head on the hard concrete. He stood up over me, then almost casually, kicked me hard in the side, making me curl in a ball. I really didn't notice him walking away. I was concentrating on getting air. On my side, at least the blood wasn't flowing into my mouth. I was able to cough up most of what had gone down my windpipe, and while still wracking with coughs, at least I was able to fill my lungs again.

Almost by force of will, I was able to calm down and simply breathe. I was not doing well. I hurt all over, and any movement brought more pain. But I was almost able to ignore the pain while I concentrated on slow, steady breaths. Eventually, I caught my breath and could just lie there, trying to catalogue where I was hurt and to what extent. From our training, I knew that the best time to escape was as soon as possible after being captured, and I needed to know what limitations I had. I knew my leg had a hole in it, and I knew my face was banged up pretty bad. But what else did I have going on?

Being tied up, though, made it difficult to figure that out. If I had my hands free, I could feel and probe. But as I was, it was almost as if I had to feel from the inside out. Pulling and flexing against the bonds around my wrists, I could feel a sharp pain in my chest. I knew my ribs were hurt, maybe broken.

While I was trying to figure out what else might be wrong with me, footsteps approached again. I felt a surge of panic and looked up. A young guy, vaguely familiar, reached down and picked up the hood that was lying beside me. He looked back at the others for a moment while they shouted at him, then bent down to put it back over my head. Just as the hood covered my eyes, it dawned on me where I had seen him before. He was the young Iraqi prisoner I had guarded just a couple of months ago back in camp.

## Chapter 12

*Somewhere in Iraq*
*Evening of July 3? Early morning of July 4, 2006?*

We moved twice during the night. Each time, I had duct tape placed over my mouth. The first time I almost died, as my swollen nose was too smashed up for air to get through. As soon as they taped my mouth, they threw the hood back on and picked me up to carry me, but my panic and writhing were so violent that they couldn't hold me and dropped me to the ground. Just before I passed out, someone must have realized what the problem was because the hood was taken off and a knife used to cut a slit in the tape over my mouth. The fact that my lips were cut as well was inconsequential. I could breathe.

"No talk," one Iraqi whispered to me, holding the knife to my throat before putting the hood back on.

I got the message. I didn't make a sound as they carried me out and threw me into the trunk of a car. They shoved my knees up almost to my chin to get me to fit, and all sorts of things dug into my back and side as we lurched to wherever we were going. The pain in my face had dulled to a continual ache, the position I was in made my back spasm several times, and I was afraid my leg was in bad shape as well.

We drove for about 30 minutes. In the movies, the hero can count time and turns to have an idea of where he was being taken; in real life, that was beyond me. I could hear other traffic, and once when we stopped, I could hear voices outside.

Part of me wanted to try and yell out through the duct tape, to make some sort of noise. But I remembered the threat, and I didn't even know who would have heard me. I felt somewhat ashamed, though, for not trying. Was I a coward?

When we arrived at our destination, I was hauled out of the trunk, my bad leg banging on the edge of it, bringing out an involuntary gasp. That earned me a backhand to the side of my face. For once, my nose didn't take the brunt of it, and compared to what I'd already experienced, this one wasn't much.

I was still hooded, but I could tell I was taken up some steps and into a building. I was dropped on the floor while my captors started talking to someone there. The tone of the conversation got more and more strident. Whoever's house this was evidently was not happy with our presence. The yelling got louder and more pointed, but finally, the homeowner evidently won. There were more shouts that sounded like orders, and I was picked up again and taken back down to the trunk and thrown inside.

Carrying me face down like that, someone on each arm and leg, was not only uncomfortable, but it was painful. Walking or hobbling might have hurt less. I wondered if I could get them to let me at least hop, but on the other hand, the more of an invalid they thought me, the better chance I would have if any opportunity presented itself.

While in the car for the second time, another issue came up. I wasn't sure just what day it was or how long I'd been held captive. I figured I'd been moved at least once while I was unconscious, but at a minimum, it was at least 10 or 12 hours since the ambush. I hadn't eaten nor had anything to drink during that time, but now, my bladder was making noises of its own. I had to piss. The bouncing around in the trunk of the shockless car was not helping. We drove for another 20 or 30 minutes, then stopped. I heard the doors open, then shut, then nothing. Outside, there were the faint sounds of a city at night, but I was still in the trunk, my bladder getting more and more insistent on relief. Finally, I couldn't take it anymore. I tried to shift my body a bit so at least I was sort of pointing down, then I let go.

Whatever had slowed down my bodily functions for the last 12 hours disappeared with a vengeance. I let loose like a racehorse. I felt relief, but also shame, as my trou kept the hot wetness against my body. I couldn't tell with just my hip and leg, but I imagined a pool of piss surrounding me. I was almost glad that my nose was beyond smelling anything at the moment.

It took awhile, but finally, the trunk was opened, and hands reached in to grab me. One man grabbed my leg, then recoiled with a shout of disgust. I could hear people jostling around the trunk, then shouts of anger. I thought I heard the sound of someone getting hit, then hands grabbed me and pulled me out. This time, instead of a person on each arm and leg, I only had someone on each of my arms. They dragged me, face up, into a building, down some stairs, and dropped me on the ground. A few minutes later, I was pulled to the sitting position. My hands were freed and the hood taken off. My hands had been tied in back of me for at least a number of hours, and as I tried to bring them forward, they didn't respond so well to my intentions. The duct tape was ripped off my mouth and the young guy, the teenager who had been our prisoner, stood by with a bucket of water.

The first guy said something in Arabic, then motioned at my crotch, then at the bucket. I got it. I nodded my understanding while trying to rub some life back into my arms. The teen placed the bucket beside me.

I finally got some motion back into my arms. I took the bucket and poured some water into my lap, then did the best I could to wash myself. My utilities had been soaked with piss as well, and I did the best I could to rinse them. I didn't use all the water for that, though. I took some of it to gingerly wash my face, trying to feel how much damage there was.

It was pretty dark in the room, and while I could hear talking on the floor above me and people walking about, only three Iraqis were in the small room with me. All three watched me wash, their faces nearly expressionless. As I washed my face, I tried to drink some of the water, but the head honcho slapped my hands away, motioning for me to continue washing. I really needed to drink, but he was the one with the weapon, not me.

When I finished, the teenager brought me a bottle of water. This was the exact same bottle as we used on base, filled by our own water plants. I wondered if that was a coincidence or was this really USMC water. I gulped the entire thing down.

After finishing it, the third Iraqi motioned for me to unbutton my trou.

*What the fuck was he going to do?*

Hesitantly, I unbuttoned, but I was not going to take my dick out no matter what. He didn't press the issue, but he placed a cracked but serviceable bowl beside my hip. He pantomimed turning over on his side and taking his dick out to piss. I guess they weren't too happy with me pissing my pants. I nodded my understanding.

The first guy then pushed my head forward, exposing my back. I wanted to resist, but my resolution to look more of an invalid that I was kept me complacent. He pulled my arms in back of me, then tied them. The hood came back on.

I wondered how they expected me to use that bowl if I was tied and hooded. And what about if I had to take a shit? What would I do then? I hoped to God that my fellow Marines would come to my rescue before that happened.

I heard the three move off to the back of the room. I knew I probably still reeked. I tried to get at least somewhat comfortable, and much to my surprise, I nodded off to sleep.

# Chapter 13

*Iraq*
*July 4, 2006*

I woke up to the smell of coffee. For a moment, I thought I was back home, Sig having gotten up to fix my breakfast. I even smiled before my senses caught up with my reality. I was on my side, arms tied behind me and numb, my leg, back, and face aching. The hood over my head couldn't keep all the light out; some came right through the fabric. It was probably late morning.

Subdued voices spoke in Arabic from several meters away. I decided to just lay still. I wasn't sure what I could glean by listening. We'd had rudimentary classes in Arabic before we deployed, but to be frank, I had pretty much forgotten all of it. I couldn't pick out anything, even the name of a city. With the amount of time I was out, I could be anywhere in the country by now.

I shifted my position slightly and that must have alerted my guards as they stopped talking. I froze, but footsteps approached, then my hood was taken off. I blinked and tried to focus on the man standing over me.

He said something to me, but of course I didn't understand. I shook my head.

He was an unremarkable-looking guy. Take away the AK slung over his back and put him in a pair of Levis and a T-shirt, he wouldn't have looked out of place at any Starbucks back at home. Clean-shaven, about 5'10" or so, I would guess, he didn't look like what I pictured an Al Qaeda terrorist would look like.

He turned to the others and said something before walking back. The young teen, the same one I'd stood guard over, was still one of my guards. He came over with a bottle of water and what looked like a piece of bread in his hands. Suddenly, my stomach growled. I hadn't eaten for at least a day, maybe more.

He stared at me stupidly, then looked back to the others and shouted out something in a questioning voice. One of the others shouted back at him, annoyance obvious even to me. The young boy turned back, then knelt in front of me. He held out the bread to my mouth, and I eagerly took a bite. This wasn't soft white loaf—this was some sort of hard, stale-tasting bread. I was starving, but I couldn't wolf it down. My mouth was too dry. I swallowed what I could, then used my chin to point at the water bottle in his other hand. He jerked back a few inches like I was attacking him, then looked at me without comprehension. Another voice yelled out, catching his attention. He looked back as he got his instructions, then nodded. Putting the bread down on the ground, he unscrewed the cap of the water bottle, then lifted it up to my lips. I think half of the water failed to make it in my mouth and instead dribbled down my chin, but I did manage to swallow a good bit.

After the bottle was empty, I tried to use my chin again to point at the bread. This time he understood, and he picked it up and pushed it into my mouth. I got a few bits of dirt or something along with it, but I didn't care. I needed the calories. The fact that they were feeding me was also a relief in and of itself. They wouldn't be feeding me if they planned on killing me, right?

I looked up at the boy. He seemed pretty nervous to me. I had previously thought he might be 16 years old or so, and that still seemed about right. I'd seen tough teenage kids back in Orange County and LA, so it wasn't just his age that made him look out-of-place. I thought he just didn't have it in him to be a fighter. The way he kept looking back at the others only reinforced my assumption. I wondered what he was doing here with the others, with an AK strapped to his back.

Of course, with me trussed up like a hog, I'm not sure what he expected me to do. If this was Hollywood, then John Rambo or John McClane would figure out something, but this was Iraq. I was hurt and tied up. I may have outweighed the kid by a hundred pounds, but there really wasn't much I could do at that moment.

He got up and left me there. I tried to pull against the bonds that held my wrists together. I didn't expect to really break them, but I needed to get some blood flowing. I knew about things like gangrene, and I was afraid that too long like this could bring it on. I wasn't sure just how long was too long.

Having something to occupy my mind was good, though. I could feel an undercurrent of fear, of panic, just roiling around under the surface of my thoughts. I knew my fellow Marines were out there looking for me, but I also knew that these Iraqis here held all the right cards. Even if a platoon of infantry assaulted this place to get me back, a simple knife across the throat would take care of my momma's favorite son. I needed to keep this fear at bay. I needed to push it down deep inside and encapsulate it, keep if from boiling out to the surface. I had to keep calm, so focusing on my arms gave me a point of reference. It gave me something other to think about.

For the next hour or so, I pulled against my bonds, both those around my wrists and those around my ankles. I tried to feel where I was hurt and to what extent. If the opportunity arose for me to make a break for it, I had to know what worked and what didn't.

My calf responded to my movements. It hurt, and I was afraid of infection, but it seemed to move OK as near as I could tell. I hoped the bullet just passed through and didn't nick the bone or tendons.

My back and side ached considerably, both from getting shot and from getting kicked. I think my flak jacket had saved me from the round itself, but when I took a deep breath, I don't know if I felt my ribs grating or if that was just my worst-case scenario imagination. Each breath hurt, but I couldn't exactly tell why.

There wasn't much I could do about my face. My nose was swollen and very sore. I could feel my pulse as it tried to push blood through the damaged tissue. I had one obviously chipped tooth. As far as anything else like a concussion, I really didn't have a clue. I thought my mind was functioning fine, but if it wasn't, would I even recognize that?

It wasn't until then that I realized the date; that is, unless I had been out an entire 24 hours earlier. It was July 4th. This was a hell of a way to spend our nation's birthday.

# Chapter 14

*Iraq*
*July 5, 2006*

I had been basically lying in the same spot for a day-and-a-half. I'd been fed twice and given water three times. They had untied my hands twice so I could piss when they realized that me just rolling over to my side would mean piss soaking all over the concrete floor. No one came in to relieve my three guards, but several times, other Iraqis came in to check out the captive American. My stress level was rising the more I was ignored. I didn't know their plans for me, and my imagination was running rampant. I'd seen the videos of what they'd done to other prisoners, and those images kept running through my brain.

With no one to talk to, I named my three guards in my mind. "Gomer" was the young kid. He was constantly at the beck and call of the others, and he was the one given my bowl of piss to throw out. The second time he picked up the bowl, his AK slid off his shoulder as he stooped to clatter on the floor. He reached for it, too late by a mile, and spilled some of my piss. "Buttface" took exception to that and slapped Gomer across the back of the head, sending his AK clattering to the floor again and spilling more of the piss on his hand.

Buttface never seemed to overtly pay attention to me, but I could see that he was aware of me 24/7. I got the feeling that he was waiting for me to make a break for it. Maybe he'd seen the *Rambo* or *Die Hard* movies, too. He was quiet, but he moved with a feral efficiency that made me wonder just how dangerous he was. He was much bigger than Gomer, but I still outweighed him by a good 40 pounds at least. That didn't mean I was underestimating him if it came down to it. Of the three, something told me he was the brawler among them.

"Joe" was the third man, the one in charge of the small group. "Joe" wasn't the most creative name in the book, and it wasn't like I didn't have time to come up with something better, but to me, he seemed like an average Joe. I wondered if he had kids and a family. If he wasn't here all the time with me, I could see him putting up his weapon, then going home to a simple family dinner, his wife asking him how work was today.

Thinking of that made me think of Sig. I wondered if she knew I was MIA yet. I figured it must be the night of the 4th back there. She might be out watching the fireworks somewhere. Last year, we'd gone outside Disneyland to watch, not paying for entry, but just to park and watch the show. It was only the second time we'd spent July 4th together since we got married.

Gomer had just given me some water, and I was lying back on the ground when footsteps sounded coming down the stairs into what was mostly likely a basement. I could occasionally hear the sounds of people moving around upstairs, so the building wasn't abandoned. I guess my captors believed in hiding in plain sight.

The approaching footsteps were nothing new. So far, at least 10 Iraqis had trooped down to look at me. One guy had even tried to talk to me in broken English, but other than his name and "Boston Red Sox," I really didn't catch much else.

Four guys entered the room. Two came up to me while the other two went to talk to Joe. There was some wild gesturing and shouting. My heart was already pounding when one of the other guys cut the rope binding my legs and the two jerked me to my feet. I would have fallen had they not held me up. The first two, followed by my three guards, came up to stand in front of me. One man, an older guy with a white beard and traditional Arab robes held up a piece of paper in front of my face and read from it.

I felt my panic rising. I tried to push it back down, but I couldn't. I really didn't like the looks of this. It got worse when one of the others picked up the hood and put it over my head. I tried to crane my head back and forth in a futile attempt to keep the hood off of me, but that didn't even slow him down. Then two men holding me dragged me backwards until I felt the wall up against my back. They let go of my arms, and I started to fall. One guy grabbed me again and pulled me upright, punching me in the side of the head. He let go, and I managed to keep on my feet.

I felt nauseous, the bile rising in my throat. I knew I should make a run for it; I should try something. I didn't do anything, though, praying that something else was going to happen than what I feared. Maybe I was just going to be moved again.

I heard the steps as the men shuffled in front of me. When the butts of weapons hit the deck, I felt my panic grow.

*This couldn't be it, could it? I was worth more as a hostage, right?*

A voice called out in Arabic, and I could almost hear the rustle of men standing at attention.

When I heard the heavily accented English word "ready" get called out, I almost didn't recognize it. The leader was already at "aim" when I realized what was happening. They weren't going to use me as a hostage, for propaganda. They were going to get rid of me.

I took a faltering step forward when I heard "fire!" I fell to the ground, legs unable to keep me standing as I heard the clicks of firing pins falling on empty chambers.

There was a moment of silence before the basement erupted with laughter. I lay there, gasping for air, still not quite sure what had happened. I just knew I was still alive.

## Chapter 15

*Iraq*
*July 6, 2006*

He had a wicked smile as he slowly put his foot on my leg and stepped down. When I screamed, his smile only grew.

After my "execution" the day before, I had been mostly left alone. Gomer had given me water and spoon-fed me some rice, food I really wasn't sure I could keep down, but ate knowing I needed my strength. I had slept fitfully all night, my mind reliving the moment that I thought my life was over.

Before the execution, I really hadn't been that openly scared. I know this is pretty ridiculous: I was being held captive by insurgents who had a history of cutting off their captives' heads and putting the video of that online. That isn't to say I wasn't concerned, but deep in my heart, I expected something to happen—the Marines charging in, a ransom being paid, anything. But that charade they pulled yesterday, well, that changed me. In a way, it broke me. I was truly, deep-down, afraid. For the first time, I felt like I probably wouldn't make it out of this alive. Intellectually, I knew I had to keep positive. But knowing that and feeling that were two different things.

In the morning, after Gomer had fed me again and let me piss, the same big guy who had choked me on the first day came in. He talked with Joe and Butthead for a few moments, glancing over at me with a predatory look in his eyes. As I'd already made his acquaintance, I was wary of him. More than wary, I was afraid. I knew what he was capable of, and I didn't want anything to do with him.

After a few minutes, he very casually walked over to me. He squatted, then pulled me into a sitting position, his face inches from mine.

"*Ali Jaffer!*" he said, thumb hitting his chest. "*Ali Jaffer!*"

I didn't know what to say, so I kept quiet. That earned me a slap across my face, which made me see stars as my nose exploded in pain.

"*Ali Jaffer!*"

I realized he was telling me his name. He wanted me to know who it was who held the power over me. He wanted me to know my tormentor.

"OK, OK, Ali Jaffer. You're him," I managed to blurt. "Ali Jaffer."

He nodded, looking pleased, then let me fall back down. He stood up, said something to me in Arabic, then almost casually stepped on my right leg. While I had been lying there, my leg was more of a constant ache than a pain, but when he ground down on it, the paid was unbearable. He eased up, and I stopped screaming, my breath coming in gasps. I looked up at him, trying to defy him, but not doing too good of a job at it.

He lifted his foot again, and held it over my leg, watching me as I couldn't help but to look down at it, just waiting for it to grind back into my calf. He just started to slowly lower it when a new voice shouted out with the sound of authority. Ali, whirled around, looking ready to snarl out at whoever was interrupting his fun, but when he saw who it was, his expression changed. He gave a guilty-looking nod and stepped away from me.

I leaned back with relief, closing my eyes, not caring for a moment just who had saved me. When footsteps approached me, though, I opened my eyes and looked up. A very filthy man, barefoot and with tattered robes that did little to cover him, stood over me. Even his eyes seemed rheumy and barely functional. Only his erect and alert posture gave a sign that this man was not some beaten-down offal of mankind.

The man, who was followed by three streetwise-looking thugs, turned and walked over to Joe and Buttface. Both showed him deference, and despite my position, curiosity hit me.

Just who was this guy?

After a few minutes of quiet discussion, the new arrivals went to the stairs and climbed out of the basement. Joe said something to Gomer who then tucked in his shirt. I couldn't understand anything they were saying, but it was obvious that they were concerned and more than a little uncomfortable. What this meant for me, I didn't know.

After 30 minutes or so, a new group of people came down the stairs. In the lead was a slight man who looked like he was in his mid-30s. He was in white, traditional robes with a dagger at his side. Other than that, he wasn't armed. His goons were, though. It took me a moment to recognize them; they were the same bodyguards who had come down with the old beggar.

The new guy pulled a chair from the corner, placed it in front of me, then sat down. I looked closely at him.

*Could he be . . .?*

"You're the beggar, aren't you?" I blurted out, forgetting my situation.

That got a smile from him and he put his right hand to his forehead, then lowered it with a flourish. "Kaseem al-Gharsi," he told me.

He seemed to wait for some sort of acknowledgement. *Was I supposed to know him?*

When I didn't respond, he asked, "And you are?"

His English was perfect. I would have mistaken him for an American had I met him back home. He raised his eyebrows in a question as he waited for me to answer. I didn't want to answer, but name and rank were what they always gave in the movies. I thought the Marine Corps expected a captured Marine to give that out as well.

"Uh, Corporal Nicholas Xenakis, United States Marine Corps."

He held out his hand to the side, and one of his goons placed an ID card in his hand. He looked at it, then looked at me and nodded.

"See, that wasn't so hard. So, Nicholas, or do they call you Nick?"

I was wary. So far, no one had asked me anything. Not my name, not how many Marines were in Fallujah, what our weapons were. Nothing. I had seen enough movies to know the questions would come. I had been steeling myself to withhold any information.

Before each pump, we had been given classes on what to do if we were captured. I was surprised to learn that the Marine Corps expected you to break. There were no cyanide capsules and all that spy stuff. We were basically told to hold out as long as possible and just not voluntarily offer up information.

I was on my guard, then, waiting for the inevitable interrogation, waiting for more of the abuse I'd already experienced. But this guy, with his American accent, calmly asking my name: well, that threw me for a loop. My nickname? Was that allowed? If my name was supposed to be given, I guessed my nickname would be OK. How could that help the insurgents?

"Uh, yeah, they call me Nick."

"Nick it is then. Are you OK? Given your circumstances, I mean."

I hesitated. Was this some sort of trick question? I glanced towards the stairs where Ali had climbed out of the basement.

"Ah, yes. I should probably apologize for that," he said, obviously figuring out my thoughts. "The Prophet is clear that we cannot abuse prisoners or those under our control. There was no reason for any of that."

*What was that?*

I'd seen the videos of prisoners getting their heads cut off. I knew the Sunnis and Shia were killing each other every night, sometimes using electric drills to drill men to death. They cut off hands for stealing, right?

"But, . . ." I started before I could help myself.

"But all Muslims are barbarians, right? That is what you are thinking. If you weren't so brainwashed by your government and media, you could see that Islam is the religion of peace. We are waging a holy war, true, against the West, but that is because of your own actions. We don't bomb cities into rubble. We don't strangle the economies of other nations. It is you, the . . . ." He paused for a second before composing himself. "I'm sorry, I don't mean to lecture you here. You came to this country because your Bush ordered you here."

I thought of the suicide bombers blowing up markets, killing women and children, and that didn't seem to civilized to me. These so-called "soldiers" rarely even met us in combat. IEDs were the way they fought. I figured I shouldn't bring any of that up.

"Despite your crusaders, we are really brothers under the same god, Allah-be-praised. It is the Jew who is trying to subvert both of our peoples."

I could see that this guy couldn't help himself from lecturing. But if that kept me from getting interrogated, all the better. I would listen to him spout his propaganda all day long if it kept him busy. I wasn't on my school debate team, but even I could pick holes in his views. If Christians and Muslims shared the same god, well, didn't the Jews have the same god, too? Even my priest back home acknowledged that us, the Protestants, the Roman Catholics, the Muslims, the Jews, they all had the same god. Just some people have perverted the Word.

"Well, no matter now. What we need to decide at the moment is what to do with you. Allah, praise-be-his-name, has seen fit to deliver you into our hands. You will be a tool for his glory, but your personal conditions and your future will depend on you, not us."

"I can't cooperate with you," I mustered up as much bravado as I could. "I'm a US Marine, and I won't betray my country."

He actually laughed. "You think I'm going to torture you to find out how many toilets you have at your base? We have loyal men and women working there. We know everything there is to know about it. I don't care about all of that. What I do care about is how to use you. At the moment, that does not include physical abuse."

I couldn't help but to look down at my leg, bloody and swollen.

"That brute is an Iraqi," he told me with a shrug as he caught the focus of my gaze. "Most of them do not understand the cause, and they don't understand how a Muslim man acts. You can blame that on the infidel Hussein. But with our guidance, they will be brought back into the arms of the Prophet."

That took me aback. I knew that Al Qaeda in Iraq had foreigners running it, but I just assumed this guy, this Kaseem whatever-he-said-his-name-was, was Iraqi, too.

He took that moment to lean over and lightly touch my leg. I jerked back the best I could, still being tied up, but he merely seemed to be checking it out.

"I will get a doctor in to take a look at that. We don't need you dying from an infection," he said matter-of-factly.

He stood up, and I sensed our little chat was over. I decided to take a chance.

"Um, can I ask you something?"

I could see his eyes harden for a moment, but he seemed to push that aside and nodded.

"When I was, uh, when I was captured, there was another Marine with me. Is he OK?"

He shrugged his shoulders as if my question was inconsequential. "The Iraqis killed six of your soldiers, and probably him, too. I will ask if you really want to know."

With that, he turned and left, his bodyguards, I guess they were, joining him and walking up the stairs. My heart fell as I watched him leave. I knew Tony had been pretty bad off, but to have it confirmed just broke my heart.

## Chapter 16

*Iraq*
*July 7, 2006*

Kaseem was as good as his word. After he left, Joe, Buttface, and Gomer milled about, studiously ignoring me. An hour or so later, a doctor, or at least I assumed he was a real doctor and not a nurse or a vet or something, was escorted in by one of Kaseem's bodyguards, a quiet, hulking man who never said a word in my presence.

The doctor was an older guy, and he checked out my leg first. He shook his head, then got some forceps and some gauze and proceeded to clean the wound. When I say clean, I mean, he stuck that thing inside the bullet hole. That was as bad as any of the beatings I had taken so far. At one point, I must have twisted, and he angrily jerked my leg back out straight.

Despite my agony, I was surprised at his attitude. I thought doctors were full of compassion and shit like that. But he seemed angry at being there. I wondered if he was forced to come, and if he thought that put him in danger.

He finally finished my leg, then checked my ribs and my face. He cleaned up the latter, ignored my still-swollen nose, then put a thin Band-Aid on the gash. I would have expected I would have needed stitches. He gave me a shot, which I hoped was antibiotics.

He stepped back and said something to Joe, who was hovering over his shoulder while he worked. Without even looking back at me, he picked up his small black leather case and walked out.

Joe tied me back up. Whatever Kaseem had wanted changed, I guess that didn't include more freedom of movement. It seemed that he wanted his prize in good condition but not to have a chance at escape. I'm not sure how I could have managed that even if I wasn't tied. I had three full-time guards, and my leg was not only swollen and infected, it now ached even more from the good doctor's administration.

Buttface had to untie my hands 30 minutes later when they brought my food. I think they realized it would be easier for all concerned for me to feed myself than being spoon-fed like a baby. I had the same rice as before, but there was also a small ground-meat thing, like a long meatball. I wondered if that was Kaseem's doing. Probably. Buttface stood over me with his AK, then tied me back up when I was done. While I was eating, he had his weapon at the ready, but to tie me back up, he slung the rifle over his shoulder. Neither Joe nor Gomer were covering him. I wasn't in any condition to try and take him, but knowing that none of the three seemed to have any real training was something to store in the back of my mind.

An hour or so later, Kaseem came back. He spoke to Joe first, then came back over as one of his bodyguards brought a chair over for his use. He sat, looked down at me and started to say something before he quit and told one of his hovering posse something. One of them, the one with the big long beard, went upstairs, then came down a few moments later with another chair. He handed his rifle to one of the other guys, then came forward, placing the chair beside me. He untied my hands and motioned me to sit. The fact that he gave his weapon up before coming to me showed me that these guys, at least, were better trained than the Three Stooges. I may have been bigger than Kaseem, but I was pretty obviously in bad shape, and my feet were tied. He had the big bodyguard with him, a guy who probably outweighed me by 25 pounds, none of it looking like fat, another guy, this one who just oozed with lethality, and an older guy who stared at me with frank hate-filled eyes: his little group of thugs looked pretty capable. Still, he was taking no chances.

"The doctor says your leg is infected, but you should start to see an improvement in a day or so," Kaseem told me once I was seated and looking at him. I didn't reply, and he went on, "If it doesn't get better, I have asked Hammad to let me know and we'll bring the doctor back."

He must have seen the question in my eyes, because he added, "Hammad. Your keeper here."

"Oh, you mean Joe," I blurted out without thinking.

"Joe? Who's Joe?"

I could tell he was confused. I sheepishly pointed over to Joe where he was hovering by the table in the corner of the room with the other two.

Kaseem was still puzzled, but then he tilted his head back and laughed. This was the first time I had heard any laughter in several days, and it echoed in the concrete basement.

"'Joe?' Why did you pick 'Joe?'" he asked.

I felt embarrassed. Which, given my situation, seemed odd.

"Uh, well, 'Joe Average' is how he seemed to me."

He gave a sort of harrumph and said, "Hammad, or Joe, if you want, is decidedly not 'average.' He is quite well educated and was a high-ranking civil servant in Hussein's regime. Now he is showing his loyalty by serving where we need him." He paused, before leaning forward and going on. "What about the other two?" he asked in almost a conspiratorial tone.

"Well, uh, . . . ," I hesitated not wanting to give any offense. I gulped and continued, "The other one is 'Buttface,' and the kid is 'Gomer.'"

His eyes widened, and I thought I might have pissed him off, but then he laughed even louder and longer. He had actual tears in his eyes when he stopped and looked back down at me.

"Well, you probably got 'Buttface' about right. I might have called him 'Asshole' myself. But why 'Gomer?'"

"You know, like he's a Gomer. I don't know how to describe it."

He shrugged and said, "I may have lived in the US, but I guess I couldn't learned everything. No matter." He paused for a few moments before going on. "What about me? Have you given me a name?"

Actually, I hadn't. He spoke English, and it never occurred to me.

"You gave me your name," I told him. "Kaseem."

"Eh, just as well, I guess. I would have hoped for something heroic like 'Lion of Allah' or something, and I doubt you would go in that direction."

As I sat there, I realized how surreal things had become. I was a prisoner of war, one not protected by the Geneva Convention. I had been tortured and abused. I had three very efficient-looking guards watching over me, and then the Three Stooges trying to look useful, too. Yet here I was, with some sort of high insurgent muckety-muck, chatting about nicknames as if nothing was wrong.

"If your leg doesn't get better, tell Hammad. We don't want gangrene to set in, now do we?" He seemed to collect his thoughts before continuing. "Now, I need to ask you a few questions."

I stiffened up when I heard that.

*Here it comes!*

He didn't seem to notice my reaction as he simply asked me, "So Nick, are you married?"

*Am I married? That's what he wants to ask?*

I hesitated. I gave him my name and service. What else was I required to give? If I gave him an answer, would that giving in to the enemy?

When I didn't say anything, frozen by indecision, he looked up at me from where he had been examining his left hand and said, "I assume you know we need to report your capture to the Red Crescent. Your family needs to know that you are alive."

That threw me for a loop. We reported all our prisoners to the Red Cross, but I didn't think that the insurgents followed the same rules. They were supposed to, sure, but I had been led to believe that they paid no attention to that. On the other hand, what could it hurt? He'd probably already Googled me and knew I was married. If I told him the truth now, maybe I could get him to believe any lies I might want to tell later. I made my decision.

"Yes, I'm married," I told him.

Did I see a quick flash of triumph in his eyes?

"Any children?"

"No, me and Sig, we . . ." I started, before he held up a hand and interrupted.

"Sig and I," he said.

"What?"

"Sig and I. Not 'me and sig.' Go on," he said.

I looked at him in confusion. An Arab is telling me how to speak English? What the fuck did it matter?

I shook my head, then went on. "Sig and I," I said with emphasis, "haven't had the right time to have kids yet."

"Too bad. A man is not a man until he has sons to carry on. But no matter. Your wife's name is Sig. So is that short for Sigfried?"

"No, Sigrun. That's Norwegian."

"So, Sigrun Xenakis?"

"She just goes by Sig," I answered.

"OK," he said, pausing to write that down. "She'll know soon that you're alive and well."

He'd put me off-balance, that was for sure. To say I was confused would be an understatement. Here I was, a prisoner, a beat-up prisoner, but he acted like my buddy, my protector. He laughed at my nicknames. He acted like he cared if I was well. But he also came across as some sort of asshole and corrected my English. Was he just so sure of himself that he had to correct the way I spoke, and from before, what I thought of Muslims? Or was he playing some sort of mind-game with me?

For the next 30 minutes or so, he sat and asked me questions, but not about the war, the Marines, or anything like that. It was all things like how I met Sig; how good was I in sports; if LA would finally get an NFL team; was In-and-Out really that good. None of it made any sense to me. I thought he might be trying to trick me, but he never asked me anything of any importance, the best I could tell.

He finally sighed, got up, and took his leave. Two of his bodyguards left first, going up the stairs, and the third followed, but not before looking back into the room, sweeping his weapon around. I am not sure if he really thought someone could have snuck in through the solid walls intent on taking out Kaseem.

Buttface came over and tied up my hands again, but he left me sitting in the chair. At least that was better than lying on my side. I just sat there and wondered what the fuck had just taken place. I don't know what I thought being a prisoner might be like, but I know it wasn't this.

# Chapter 17

*Iraq*
*July 7 or 8, 2006*

I was drifting off when Gomer shook me awake. I came to with a start, and that caused Gomer to jump back. Only one of the two lights in the basement was on, but as there were no windows to the outside, I had to guess that it still must be nighttime.

I almost laughed at Gomer's typical jumpiness, but then I saw Joe, Buttface, and two other Iraqis standing by. Anything out of the ordinary was enough to get my heart pounding. Then I saw Buttface holding a roll of duct tape. I pushed back with my still-tied feet until my back was up against the wall.

Buttface followed me, pulling out one edge of the tape until he had some free. I started to squirm when he reached forward, but with the wall in back of me, there was nowhere for me to go. He slapped the tape over my mouth and nose as I turned my head. With both covered, I froze, not able to drawn in a breath. Buttface continued to wrap the tape around my head until someone shouted out and he stopped, then took the tape back off until my face was uncovered. Relief swept over me.

He put his hand on my head and turned it so I was facing him, giving it a shake and saying something sharply to me. He held the tape up in front of me, showing me it was coming back on. I got the message. He was going to tape me up no matter what, and if I wanted my nose free, I had better keep still.

The swelling in my nose had gone down some. I just hoped it was enough for me to get enough air in. It wasn't like I had any choice though, so I held still as he wrapped the tape around my head several times.

I tried to calm myself down, knowing it would help me breathe. I found out that if I controlled my breathing, I could in fact get air through my nose. The swelling had gone down enough for that.

After the tape, Joe came up and put a hood over my head. That almost brought the panic back. I hoped the hood wouldn't cut off the oxygen.

Hands grabbed me under my arms and got me to my feet. They started to pull me forward, but as my feet were still tied, I fell on my face. This seemed to surprise them, although I don't know what they expected me to do while bound like that. After a long discussion, I felt myself being bodily picked up and carried to the stairs. We clumped up it with them half-dropping me twice. I just concentrated on staying calm.

I could hear the difference in the footsteps as we got upstairs. We walked over tile or something, then what had to be carpets and the sound of the steps became subdued. I realized that we were probably inside someone's house. What family wanted a prisoner kept in their basement, I wondered.

When I could feel a breeze against me, I knew we were outside. It wasn't a cool breeze. No light came in through the hood, so that confirmed it was night, but this was July, and even the desert night still retained heat. Still, it was the first breath of air I had felt since I had been brought here.

I heard the sound of a sliding door open, like on a van. I momentarily contemplated trying to squirm to the ground, but I realized that would do me no good at all, so I meekly kept limp as they pushed me into the van. I was pushed along the floor until I fell into a depression and someone reached in to fold my legs up against my chest. Something was then put on top of me, holding me down. I realized they must have put me into some sort of secret compartment. I tried pushing up to get a feel of my small prison, but as I was on my side, I couldn't get much leverage. Then I felt a small but very sharp prick in my side. I froze. It was a knife, I knew. Above me, there was one of my captors, and he was holding a knife through a slot or something, holding it against me. They wanted me to know that any trouble from me, and the knife would be pushed home.

The van started, and we drove off. I still had no idea where I was. I guessed I could still be in Fallujah, but more likely, I was already pretty far from there. Fallujah was generally in US hands, so someplace like Ramadi or some of the smaller villages would be a better guess.

We drove for about 10 minutes until we came to a stop. I could hear voices outside, then others answering from inside the van. The door pulled open, and several people in the van spoke. I tried to figure out if this was a checkpoint or more insurgents. Suddenly, I thought I heard a voice in English. I couldn't be sure, but the cadence and sound of it, even as muffled as it was, didn't sound like Arabic.

Even with the tape, I knew I could make some noise, I could draw some attention. I had just about made up my mind to try when the knife point went in a little deeper. In my excitement, I had forgotten about that, as hard as that might seem to fathom. But the message was received. If I made any noise at all, my life would end right here in this van. For another moment, I wondered if that would be worth it, though. Maybe I should end it. But I wasn't ready to die, so I just remained quiet. The van door closed, and we drove off again. Another five minutes, ten minutes, I don't know, we stopped. The panel above me was removed, and hands dragged me out. I was carried once more into a building, then down some steps. I could hear the guys carrying me grunting and groaning, gasping for air as they lugged me. I was dropped unceremoniously on the floor where I lay quiet until someone took off my hood. Buttface took out a knife to cut off the tape on my mouth.

Actually, he had held the knife in front of my face, slowly turning it. I knew he was trying to get a rise out of me, but they didn't move me in the middle of the night just to find someplace else to kill me. I paid him no attention until he cut off the tape.

I looked around. Just another basement, slightly more narrow than the last, but pretty much the same. I might have been in a new place, but nothing had really changed.

## Chapter 18

*Iraq*
*July 11, 2006*

When I heard the footsteps coming down the stairs, I didn't think much about it. Kaseem had come the last three days to chat and see how I was. I had begun to relax around him. He never brought up anything about the military. We just talked about life and things, even good-naturedly arguing on whether football or soccer was a better sport. Just typical guy things. He didn't seem to be trying to change my mind about anything. Well, he hinted about converting, I think. He told me that during the wars with the Barbary pirates, captured sailors in Tripoli could get their freedom if they converted to Islam, as Muslims couldn't keep other Muslims prisoner. He told me that one Scottish guy converted and became their high admiral.

I didn't buy any of that, though. I knew Sunnis and Shia were killing each other every night, so what difference would it make if I converted? Not that I would, of course. I could never leave the Church.

For the last two days, he even brought me iced tea. I don't know what I appreciated more, the cold liquid flowing down my throat or the mint aftertaste. I hoped he was bringing more today.

I looked up, expecting to see Kaseem, but some new guys came into the basement, carrying some black cases. Joe went over to meet them, and after some discussion and pointing around the basement, the newcomers went to the inside wall and put the cases down.

This basement was about 20 feet long and about 15 feet wide. The stairway came down in one corner, and the short wall next to that was featureless. The long wall up against where they kept me had one very small boarded-up opening near the top that let in a tiny bit of light, and the far short wall also had the same kind of opening, but this one was boarded up more effectively, and no light came in. These were the outside walls. The wall opposite from me had no openings other than the stairwell coming down. I assumed that this was an inside wall with the other side being either dirt or another room.

The four men opened up the cases, ignoring me. My heart sank, though, when I saw what they were unpacking. First, out came industrial lights, four sets. I was puzzled by this for a moment until one of the men set up a tripod and put a video camera on it.

I'd seen videos of prisoners before. I think all men and women going to Iraq had searched for them on the internet before we came. We'd seen the horrific beheadings.

I looked at my guards. Gomer and Joe looked nervous. I'd been with the three men basically 24/7 for the last six days. They only left to go upstairs for a few minutes at a time, probably to take a piss or whatever. They ate and slept in the basement. No one relieved them so they could go home. As such, I was beginning to be able to read them, I thought. And I didn't like what I saw in those two. Gomer, in particular, looked upset, and he kept looking over at me.

Once the lights and the camera were set up, two of the new men left, and the others just hung out for a good half an hour. All ignored me. Finally, one looked at his watch, then took a chair and set it up against the inside wall. The other guy turned on the lights, making me squint. These were industrial work lights, not klieg lights or anything like that, but after a couple of days in semi-darkness, they were plenty bright. I was pulled to my feet and crow-hopped over to the chair. My leg infection was in fact getting better, and most of the pain was surprisingly gone, but I acted like it hurt much more than it really did.

I was sat down where I waited. I couldn't help but to look around to see if anyone had a large sword or knife. They didn't need anything large, though. I'd seen the video proof of that. Once again, I started wondering if this was finally it. Was I destined to die today, fodder for some propaganda video? Would my friends see it? My family? Would Sig see it, and would she even care?

I heard the footsteps coming back down, and when I saw Kaseem, relief flooded me. He wouldn't let anything happen to me, I knew. I even broke out into a smile.

"Kaseem, what's going on? What's happening?" I asked him as he came up.

His eyes hardened ever so slightly, but I didn't care. I was just happy to see him.

"Nothing much, Nick. We just need to prove that you are alive. We need to video you and send that out. There have been reports that you were executed, which is all propaganda gamesmanship. You don't look executed to me, right?" he asked as a smile took over his face.

I obviously knew that they were going to tape me, and I was relieved that it wasn't going to be something more final. I really didn't want to make any video, but I guessed it would be OK just to show I was alive. If nothing else, it would keep my fellow Marines looking for me. They wouldn't give up the search.

"That's probably OK, then," I said.

He spent the next few minutes putting people into position. I was sitting on the chair, of course. The Three Stooges were in back of me. One of the new guys was on the camera with the other one beside him. Kaseem's posse was in back of those two. As far as Kaseem, he had on a new type of robe, more like what the Iraqis wore, but his face covered up. None of the Three Stooges had his face covered.

Joe had a piece of paper in his hands. After Kaseem told the cameraman to roll them or whatever you say in Arabic, Joe started reading from the paper. I was surprised at that. I wondered why Kaseem didn't read it instead of just standing there in complete anonymity. When Joe stopped, there seemed to be an expectant air about the rest. Everyone just stood around for a few moments before Kaseem got flustered and shouted at one of his goons. The big guy came forward fumbling at his pocket before bringing out another sheet of paper. Kaseem snatched it out of his hands and gave it to me.

"Put that down for now, then after Hammad finishes, lift it up and read from it."

I wanted to take a look at it first, but Kaseem was already getting the camera rolling again. I held it in my hands, which were still tied, and looked up into the camera while Joe did his thing. When he finished, I almost looked back at him, but I kept looking forward and raised the paper up—and couldn't read a thing. The lights were in my eyes, and my hands were tied. I could see some writing, but it was scrawled rather poorly, and with the lights, I just couldn't see anything.

"I can't see what I'm supposed to say," I said, turning to Kaseem. "The lights are too bright, and I can't read this."

I held up my tied hands with the paper flopping over them. I thought he was going to explode, but he gave out some orders, and the lights were shifted and my hands freed.

In the two previous takes, he had been on the end of the four of them with Buttface on one end and Gomer and Joe in the middle. Both Buttface and Gomer were armed with their AKs. Evidently, Kaseem thought he could control things better if he was in the middle, because he reached over to pull Gomer back.

The explosion seemed louder due to the confined space in the basement. I wasn't sure what had happened, but several people ducked to the ground while plaster and cement dust rained down on us. My ears were ringing.

Slowly, the others got up. Gomer was scared shitless, I could tell. He had accidentally fired his weapon when Kaseem grabbed him. He looked at Kaseem, his mouth open, as he tried to stutter something out. Kaseem took the weapon from his nerveless hands, then in a sudden move, buttstroked the boy alongside his head. Gomer went down in a heap while Kaseem calmly took out the magazine, removed the rounds, then put the empty magazine back in the rifle. He kicked Gomer in the side to get him up. The buttstroke he had given was at an angle to Gomer's head; it wasn't intended to take him out, just hurt. Gomer got up, eyes wide in fear. Blood trickled from the side of his head.

Kaseem gave him back his now unloaded rifle. He had one of his posse bring a rag and wipe the blood, then told him to change sides with Buttface, obviously so that the blood would not show if it started oozing again.

I was in a mild state of shock. That buttstroke did not fit the Kaseem I'd come to know. I guessed every man has a breaking point, and his had been reached. He was evidently over it, though, as he calmly turned to the others to get this thing taped again.

Once again, Joe went through his spiel, and this time, when it was my turn, I held up the paper and could see.

"My name is Corporal Nicholas Xenakis, United States Marine Corps. I was captured in Fallujah on July 3, 2006 by Iraqi freedom fighters."

The "freedom fighters" almost gave me pause, but I went on.

"Since my capture, I have been treated well."

Again, "well" was hardly an accurate description.

"I have received medical treatment for my wounds. As a US citizen, I am opposed to the policy of my government that . . . ."

I stopped reading and looked up at Kaseem.

"I can't say this," I told him.

I could see him trying to retain control.

"No, you're wrong, and you will say it. You know it's the truth, and your testament is Allah's will, praise-be-his-name."

"But Kaseem, I can't say this, and you know the Geneva Convention says I don't have to."

I don't know what la-la-land I was living in. I don't know what I thought. But I was not prepared for Kaseem motioning to one of his goons, the lethal-looking guy. He sauntered over and reached down to me. I thought he was going to take the paper, but instead, he grabbed my right forefinger, and with one twist, broke it.

The surprise as much as anything else made me scream. I looked down at my finger, which now stood upright between the knuckle and the first joint. I felt faint. I looked up at Kaseem, and he just stood there, no expression on his face. He didn't look angry; he didn't look sorry. It was then that I realized I meant nothing to him. This was no more than someone stepping on an ant.

"You will read it," was all he said.

I felt my anger rise. I would not give in to him.

"Fuck you!"

He remained expressionless and merely nodded at his goon again. The man reached down and took my middle finger, snapping it as well. I was expecting it, but the pain almost overwhelmed me. I didn't want to look at it, but some sort of morbid curiosity overcame me. My middle finger now stood up, but with my hand flat. With all the pain, all I could think of was that I could not flip him the bird now.

I looked up at him, trembling with pain and rage, determined to not give him the satisfaction of winning. He must have seen it in my eyes because he shrugged, motioning his henchman back.

*I had won!*

"Farid" was all he said.

I wondered what that meant, but then the big bodyguard came forward, holding something rolled like the tool cases that come with a new car. He put it on the ground in front of me and unrolled it, revealing things that shook me to my core.

"No more fingers. I need those to look whole in front of the camera, but we can pan it up so that anything below the waist isn't seen," he said in English, although he seemed to be addressing Farid. Then he turned to look into my face. "You will find that Farid is quite skilled at what he does."

I tried to swallow, but my throat was seizing up. I watched in horror as Farid seemed to contemplate his tools. Almost daintily for such a big man, he pulled out a small electric drill. He motioned to his two compatriots who came forward and undid the bindings on my feet, then took off my pants. All the time, he stood in front of me, turning on and off the drill. I could feel my utilities being taken off, but the drill was all I could see.

Without any expression, he leaned forward and let the turning drill bit gently kiss the skin on my left thigh, not breaking the surface. He looked up at Kaseem, but I was just staring at him. Kaseem must have given him the OK because he pushed forward, and the drill dug into me. I screamed again while the pain lanced through me, racing from my leg up to my brain. Everything in front of me whited out.

When I collected my thoughts again, I could hear retching. I thought it might be me at first, but almost as if I was floating over my body, I knew it was Gomer. I even felt sorry for him. That lasted all of a few seconds as Farid ran the drill into my thigh once more.

This time, he hit bone and the drill bit skittered to the side to chew up more of my muscle. I was screaming now at the top of my lungs, trying to cope with the agony.

I wasn't really aware of when he stopped. I was panting for air, my leg was on fire. I could hear the drill being turned on and off, taunting me, and the sound made my blood run cold. I didn't know if I could take much more. I should just read the stupid thing and get it over with. Everyone would understand, right?

The drill stopped and I could hear it being put away. I opened my eyes, not realizing I had had them closed. Farid was looking at Kaseem, but my eyes were firmly locked on him. Whatever Kaseem told him must have made an impact, because I could see him flinch. For the first time, something had broken his reserve. He gathered himself up and reached down. When he came up, he had a pair of pliers, one with a large gripping surface in his hands. The drill looked worse, but I knew he could crush my fingers with the pliers. I steeled myself for what was coming.

He moved closer to me. I stared into his eyes, and for a moment, I thought I saw something in there, something almost human. Then it went away, and his hand reached between my legs and grabbed one of my balls. My mind went crazy. I was thinking my fingers again, or maybe my teeth. This took me by surprise. I tried to squirm away, but the other two men were holding me tight. Still, I managed to throw the bearded guy to the ground, freeing my arm. Even in the sitting position, my punch knocked Farid on his ass, breaking the hold he had on my balls.

I started to struggle to get up, but Kaseem called out and the other three guards rushed in to hold me. The bearded guy had already jumped up and had grabbed my arm, wrenching it almost out of the socket. Farid stood up, rubbing his jaw. He didn't seem angry, but he moved forward with a new purpose.

Once again, a hand closed on my left ball. I was in a panic. I had four men holding me down, and although I could shift them, I couldn't get up. Then, my world came apart. From my groin came a volcano of fire. I stopped struggling and just melted into a slag of featureless agony. I couldn't think, I couldn't breathe, I couldn't exist. Nothing I have ever experienced could come close to what I just felt.

I don't know how much time passed. I finally started regaining what it meant to be a human being, to have thoughts of self. I slowly became aware of the others around me. As my eyes could focus, I recognized them. Gomer looked like he was going to pass out, and Joe was not much better. Buttface was on my right arm, a look of, well, of almost excitement on his face. Bearded guy was angry, and he had my left arm in a vise grip. One of the camera crew guys was holding my right leg, but he didn't look too enthused. Someone had their arm around my neck, probably the lethal guard. And Farid stood in front of me, expressionless once again.

It was Kaseem who scared me, though. I was conscious again, but the pain in my left ball had taken over all else. I could not imagine what was done to it, what it looked like. Through the pain, though, Kaseem took my attention. For once, his expression had changed, and like Buttface, there was a sense of excitement in him. Or maybe it was a sense of power.

He held out his hand, and Farid handed him the pliers. I could see the blood on them, my blood. Farid stepped back and let Kaseem move in front of me.

"Nick, Nick, see what you've done to yourself? None of this was necessary, you know. This is all your fault," he said, fake concern dripping from his voice.

"Fuck you," I tried to say, but pretty much all that came out was a mumbled gurgle.

Kaseem knew what I was saying, though. "I'm afraid, if we go on, that is one thing you'll never do again. Your Sig won't ever be satisfied with someone who is not a man, someone who cannot do his duty."

I knew I should just give in. I should just agree. But I couldn't let the bastard win. This had gone beyond my country, beyond the Corps. This was between him and me.

"Last chance, Nick," he said, opening and shutting the pliers in front of me.

I felt a rush of strength. I said nothing.

"Very well. As you wish."

He reached down and grabbed my remaining ball. He gave it a tug, sending shocks of pain from my destroyed one. That strength I felt a moment ago fled like rats on a sinking ship.

"With no children, no man is whole. His life is wasted. But maybe not every man deserves to breed, so I guess it's OK."

As I felt more than saw the pliers go in, I broke. I utterly, totally broke.

"OK, OK! I'll say whatever you want me to say! For the love of God, just stop!" I cried out.

"Ah, excellent, Nick. Good decision," he said with what had to be satisfaction at having won, but maybe with bit of regret coloring his voice.

I was sobbing for my inner manhood lost, even as I had saved my physical manhood.

# Chapter 19

*Iraq*
*July 12, 2006*

*I am opposed to the policy of my government that has sent me here to invade Iraq.*

The words kept running through my head.

*I, and my fellow soldiers, have killed women and children, under orders from George Bush.*

*I am a war criminal.*

I had read more, but all along the same lines. I had broken so completely that I read the words put in front of me, not caring, only wanting the agony to end. Now, though, shame washed over me. What kind of man was I to admit to lies like that?

The last 24 hours had to be about the worst of my life. The pain I suffered was almost unbearable, but breaking my spirit like that: well, that *was* unbearable. That was worse than the torture.

After the taping, everyone packed up and left, leaving me with my three guards. Joe and Gomer helped me up and basically carried me over to my place against the wall. They laid me down, then Gomer came back with some water. I tried to drink, but I retched it right back up, each spasm sending jolts of pain from my balls to my brain. I wasn't sure how long I lay there, but at some point—an hour, three hours, five hours, I don't know—the doctor came back.

Once again, he didn't say anything to me, he didn't look me in the eye. I was just a broken piece of meat to him. He looked at my fingers first, then with a quick move, wrenched them straight. That was worse than the breaking, but I didn't have the energy to scream out with much force. He taped the two fingers together.

When he shifted his attention to my balls, spreading my legs, Gomer suddenly puked, some of it splashing on me. He turned and ran back to the far side of the basement.

For once, I saw an expression on the doc's face. It wasn't pity, though. It was more like annoyance. He pursed his lips and his eyebrows scrunched together. He reached down and touched the swollen mass that my nutsack had become, but without trying to cause more pain, I think. He shook his head, then reached into his bag and brought out a scalpel.

I started to panic again. I tried to get up, and he called out for Joe and Buttface to hold me down. Before, I had been able to throw Kaseem's men around somewhat, but now, I was as weak as a kitten. They had no trouble immobilizing me.

The doctor reached down with the scalpel and made a quick incision. It hurt, to be sure, but not nearly as bad as I expected. I didn't even shout out, only gasped. When he reached in with his hand, though, it was worse. He didn't seem to be trying to hurt me, but a hand inside your nutsack, maneuvering a ruined ball, well, no way that can be done gently. He was quick, though, I'll give him that. I couldn't see what he was doing, but in five or ten seconds, seconds of pretty severe pain, he leaned back, something bloody in his hand. My mind didn't want to acknowledge what he held. I knew what it was, of course, but I refused to think about it.

He wrapped it up in a piece of paper, then moved back forward with a bottle from which he poured liquid right into the hole he'd made. It hurt like hell, but not with the same sharp intensity. Even when he took out a needle and thread, it hurt, yeah, but not that bad. Maybe that was just in comparison to what I been suffering before.

He made me take a pill, then gave the rest to Joe. They couldn't have their prize package die of infection, now, could they?

For the rest of the evening and night, I drifted back and forth, half conscious, half out of it. The words I'd spoken would not leave me. I'd been a POW for over week, and despite all that had happened to me, this was the first time I felt real despair.

Gomer got a little water down me, but I couldn't eat until morning when I was able to down a bit of rice. I didn't want it, but I knew I had to get some calories in me.

Much to my surprise, I wasn't in tremendous agony by morning. Whatever the doctor had done seemed to have had some effect. I could feel that the swelling between my legs had gone down, and while I still had a pretty serious ache there, the shooting pain that any movement had brought the day before had mostly faded. It was the same with my fingers and leg. They ached, but it was bearable. I had the feeling that if I tried to use my hand, or if I tried to bear any weight on my leg, it might be different. But just lying there, well, it somehow wasn't too bad. On the other hand, maybe I was just getting used to it.

Gomer was pretty attentive during the morning. He didn't look the worse-for-wear. Kaseem had hit him more of a glancing blow above the ear, so not much showed. He had a tiny bit of dried blood showing at his hairline, but that was about it. He kept coming up to me, offering me water. If I didn't know better, I would have thought he felt sorry for me.

It had to have been late morning sometime when Kaseem came back down into the basement. He was back in his fancy white robes and rhino horn dagger in his belt. Farid was missing, and for a moment, I hoped it was because he was suffering from when I punched him. I realized this was probably wishful thinking, though.

Kaseem nodded to me as he walked by to talk to Joe. Joe gave his report, then Kaseem came back, pulling the chair around so he could sit and face me. I involuntarily pulled back, then felt ashamed for doing that. If Kaseem noticed my flinch, he didn't give any indication of it.

"So, how goes it, Nick? You OK?"

*What the fuck?* I wondered. *How does he think I feel?*

When I didn't say anything, he sighed and went on, "OK, you're probably a little angry now. No matter. It wasn't personal."

"Not personal?" I stammered out, my surprise overcoming my desire to ignore the man.

"Of course not. I thought you were smarter than that. Yesterday, as unfortunate as it was, was merely a game being played. You were just a tool to serve Allah, praise-be-his-name, even as all of us, infidels included, are tools for him. As a friend . . ."

I almost gagged when he said "friend."

". . . I personally hated to see that. But we all have to suffer on this earth to enter Paradise."

I didn't say anything, but I just wasn't buying it. I'd seen the pleasure flash on his face after he had Farid crush my nut. I saw the look of excitement on his face when he had the pliers in his hands. I never saw any regret.

"Now, it's over. Over and done. The doctor says you'll be fine, so now just relax the best you can."

He must have seen that I was not convinced of his BS because he went on, "Look, do you know what the Qur'an says about suicide?"

I shook my head.

*He who commits suicide by throttling shall keep on throttling himself in the Hell-Fire forever and he who commits suicide by stabbing himself shall keep on stabbing himself in the Hell-Fire.*

I couldn't help myself. I looked up and asked, "So why do you guys blow yourselves up all the time?"

"The Qur'an also says:"

*And reckon not those who are killed in Allah's way as dead; nay, they are alive (and) are provided sustenance from their Lord.*

I didn't see the connection. Who said suicide was Allah's way when it sounded to me like it wasn't in his way?

"You see, sometimes we need to do what we don't want in order to serve Allah, praise-be-his-name. No man wants to kill himself, right? Yet he does it because that is how he can best serve, how he can ensure his place in Paradise. We are just tools in his name, all of us."

I could hear the sincerity in his voice. He really believed this.

"My point is because our earth is a sinful place, we sometimes have to commit sin for the greater good. We do things that would seem to be wrong, but when it is in the service of Allah, praise-be-his-name, it is no longer a sin. That part is out of our hands. We do what we have to do, and in the end, we get what we want."

"Did you get what you wanted with that video? Am I all over the internet now?" I asked bitterly.

"That video? Well, no, we didn't release that to the world. I decided to hold it for now. You were not in very good shape, as you recall, and I just thought that maybe we could wait on releasing it until it becomes necessary."

I knew then that the whole thing had been a sham. He may have sounded sincere for the last minute or so, and maybe he was, but yesterday's little event was solely to make me break, just like my fake execution. If I'd given in immediately, well, maybe they would have used the tape. But he knew I wouldn't; that's why the wording was so harsh and extreme. He wanted me to refuse so he could break me. He couldn't use the video if I was tortured, after all. A video like that had to look voluntary. I'm positive he knew about the Vietnam POWs blinking Morse code and things like that to say they were tortured. He knew videos like that were discounted. The video was not what he wanted. *He wanted me. He wanted to control me. And all of this, from the moment I was captured, was part of his plan.*

I couldn't believe I had been taken in by him. We were arguing football versus soccer, for fuck's sake. I was a prisoner, a tortured prisoner, and I thought he was my protector? What a friggin' idiot I was.

At that moment, I knew I had to fight back. I knew it before, but more as an abstract. Now I felt it in my heart. It infused my very being. To start with, I had to put on a false face, to let them think I was broken. I let a huge breath out, as if I had been hoping against hope to hear what he had just said.

"Oh, thank God! I—I didn't want my friends to see that. Thank you," I said, trying not to go overboard.

I was looking down at my feet, not meeting his eyes. I could almost hear him thinking, wondering if I was sincere.

"Well, we still have it," he said, hesitantly, "and if we need it, I can't promise that we won't release it."

Ah, the carrot and the stick. He was holding that over me. I had let that video, let what I'd said, haunt me all night. But as things became clear to me, I didn't care anymore. Release the stupid thing. I wasn't proud of it by any means, but I wasn't going to let him have another tool to use against me. I had to convince myself that it didn't matter, that I didn't care.

"Here," he told me, holding out a water bottle full of iced tea.

I knew he was my sworn enemy, but I wasn't going to turn down the tea. I settled in for what I knew was going to be an hour of inconsequential chatting about nothing important. He had to reinforce that he was my friend, my buddy, until the next time he brought the hammer down.

# Chapter 20

*Iraq*
*July 13, 2006*

Gomer sat down in front of me, a plate of rice and a couple of sections of orange in his hand. He held them out to me.

"*Farouk*," he said as I took the plate.

Rice was my staple, but I hadn't had fruit during my time in captivity. I eagerly took it.

"*Shakran*," I told him, one of the few Arabic words I remembered.

I hadn't been tied since the video, I'm guessing since they probably figured I wasn't in any shape to make a break for it. I might not have been, to be honest, but I wasn't as bad off as I would have expected.

"*Farouk*," he said again, this time pointing at himself.

Ah, he was telling me his name. Well, no matter what his real name was, he was Gomer to me.

"*Shakrun, Farouk*," I told him, watching the smile spread across his face. "Nick," I told him, shifting the plate to my right hand and pointing with my thumb to my chest.

"Nick," he parroted without too much trouble.

Buttface yelled out something at him, but Gomer flipped his hand back over his shoulder as if he was brushing off a fly. Buttface had taken off the night before. When morning came around, he was nowhere in sight, and as the morning dragged on, Joe and Gomer were getting more and more nervous. Finally, a disheveled Buttface came rushing down the stairs. Joe read him the riot act, and not five minutes later, Kaseem came by for his daily visit. I guessed Buttface got back by the skin of his teeth, and now he seemed to have lost some status among the other two. I don't think Gomer would have stood up to him before.

Gomer's whole attitude seemed to have changed. He had never been cruel to me, but now, he seemed much more considerate. He also had cooled off towards Kaseem. He still feared him, I could tell, but I also caught him stealing glances at his leader when he thought no one was looking. Those glances seemed chock-full of malice to me.

As he squatted there, watching me eat, I wondered what I could do with that. How could I use Gomer to escape from here?

# Chapter 21

*Iraq*
*July 18, 2006*

A couple of hours after I could hear the unmistakably sound of a Cobra opening up somewhere near and the sounds of small arms fire, they decided to move me again. I had heard the sounds of war several times since I'd been captured, but this was the closest. I got a little excited when I thought they could be coming for me, but when the fighting died off, I knew it was just another firefight. If the Marines knew I was here, nothing would have stopped them from reaching me.

By now, I was almost an old salt about moving. My hands were tied again, my feet hobbled. My mouth was taped and a hood was placed over my head, and with a man on each arm, I walked/hopped into a vehicle and down into a hidden compartment. My nose had healed by now, so breathing wasn't really a problem.

This time, we drove for only about five minutes, so I knew we hadn't changed towns. I just didn't know which town that was. I was taken out of the van, but instead of walking down into a basement, I was helped as we climbed three sets of stairs. The building did not have the feel of a private residence. There was too much of a feeling of emptiness, of a slight echo to our movements.

We entered what sounded like a more enclosed space. My captors asked something, and I heard Joe's voice respond. I could hear another door open as I was guided over. Suddenly, I was given a pretty forceful push, and with my legs tied, I went down hard, hitting my face on the hard ground. For once, I was grateful for the hood which had maybe saved me from a concrete road rash. My hood came off, the tape removed from my mouth, and my legs untied, but my hands were kept tied. At least they were in front of me, not behind me like when I was first captured.

I looked around at my new jail cell. This was a small room, about eight feet by eight feet. There was one window high up, but like in the last basement, it was covered over. It was nighttime, so I couldn't tell if it would let any light in during the day. The floor was concrete, and in the corner was my familiar piss bucket. That was pretty much all I could see before the door was closed, leaving me in total darkness. Unlike before, no guards were watching me. I was on my own.

At first, I reveled a bit to be alone. But after awhile sitting in the dark, I almost wished I was back in one of my other prisons. At least there, I had something to look at.

I couldn't fall asleep, so my thoughts tended to drift. I wondered what my family was going through. Did they think I was alive? Were they pressuring our congressman to do something? I wished there was some way to contact them, just to let them know. And Sig? My biggest fear was that maybe she was relieved. Our marriage was in trouble, not that I wanted to admit it. I didn't think Sig hated me or would wish me harm, but what if she welcomed the circumstances as a way out, and a way out that would garner her pity and a nice SGLI payment?

I didn't know anymore what I thought of her. I wanted our marriage to work out, but I had to admit that that could be because I didn't want to admit failure, not because of love. I thought I still loved her, but how could I know for sure sitting here in some Godforsaken Iraqi city, cut off from my entire world?

I was wallowing in self-pity when the door opened up. I blinked in the light as two Iraqis threw another bound man into the room. They unbound his feet, the removed his hood and tape, then left, shutting the door again. I don't think he saw me when he was thrown in because when I cleared my throat to speak, he called out.

"Who's there?"

He was speaking English, although not with an American accent. English was good enough for me, though.

"Corporal Nicholas Xenakis, United States Marine Corps."

"Oh, just brilliant, a bloody septic," his disembodied voice reached me through the darkness. "Sergeant Dennis Coxen, Second Battalion, the Royal Anglian Regiment, at your service."

# Chapter 22

*Iraq*
*July 19, 2006*

"And then the bloody house came down on me. I didn't know anything else until I woke up in a spider hole out in the desert somewhere."

We'd been exchanging stories on how we'd been captured. Dennis was a sergeant in the Royal Anglians, a light infantry regiment. On May 3, he'd been out on a routine patrol in Basra when they taken some fire from some Fedayeen, and he called them, who then fled the scene through an abandoned building. In hot pursuit, he'd led his squad into the building when it exploded. The whole thing had been a trap.

"I don't know what happened to my lads. When I came to, I was banged up alone."

"How'd they treat you?" I asked. As daylight broke outside, a few rays of light made it past the window covering, giving us a bit of visibility. He didn't look much worse for wear.

"Ah, the first few weeks were a mite rough. They pulled me out of that hole to beat me about and ask their questions. Most was strictly amateur. Only the Iranian bloke knew what he was doing," he told me.

"How do you know he was Iranian?" I asked.

"By his accent and his poor Arabic. I guess I didn't tell you, I speak Arabic. I worked in an Egyptian restaurant back in Leicester, and because I knew a few words, the Army sent me to school after I enlisted," he said. "I never let on to these camel jockeys, though, that I could understand them. No use giving that up."

"Poor Arabic? But you said he was Iranian."

"And Iranians speak, what . . .?" he asked.

I shrugged, then realized that he probably couldn't see me do that. "Arabic?"

I could almost hear him rolling eyes as he said, "What kind of schools do you have in the States? Iranians speak Persian."

Persian, Arabic, couldn't be much difference, I thought.

"OK, Persian. So you've got a lot of Arabs back home?" I asked, wanting to change the subject from my lack of knowledge.

"No, mostly Pakis. We've got more of them than anyplace in Blighty. But we've got our few Arabs, too.

"Where are we now, anyway? No one mentioned the city on the drive over here," he asked.

"I don't really know," I answered. "I mean, I was taken in Fallujah, but I was out pretty hard when they took me to the first place, so we could be anywhere. I think we might be in Ramadi or Haditha, though, not in some small village. Ramadi's still pretty much Indian country."

Dennis merely grunted. I'd seen Brits around and about before, but I'd never worked with them, and Dennis was the first guy I'd had a chance to talk to. Except for his accent, he could have been any other Marine. His story was pretty much the same as any of ours.

As the light had penetrated the room, something about him seemed familiar. It took awhile until it came to me. Almost every every Marine I knew had seen the old movie *Zulu*, where the British company at Rorke's Drift held off about a million Zulus. Dennis looked like the actor who played Private Harry Hook, a shitbird who earned the Victoria Cross in the battle. When I told Dennis that, he laughed.

"That guy just died last year. James Booth was his name. But you must be blind, ' cause in all modesty, I'm much better looking."

I was taking a liking to this guy. "As long as we're stuck here together, I just hope you're not the fuck-up the real Private Hook was."

"Ah, you bloody septics don't know the truth. The *Zulu* Hook was all Elstree, all Hollywood as you would call it. In real life, Hook was a teetotaler, a model soldier, and I hate to break it to you, but I'm no Harry Hook. I like my pints, I do."

"What the hell's a 'septic?' You keep saying that," I asked.

"A Yank. You know, 'septic tank, yank.' Rhyming slang. You've heard of 'apples and pears' for stairs, right?" he asked.

"No, and I don't get it."

"That's the most famous one, but we don't really use it much, not even the bloody Cockneys who invented rhyming slang. Well, you being a 'septic,'" he went on, putting emphasis on the word—if his hands weren't tied, I would have expected him to make the quote marks with his fingers as he said it— "how about 'Britney Spears' for beers. Like 'pour me a Britney Spears there, barman.'"

"That's all pretty friggin' stupid, if you ask me," I grumbled, still not entirely getting it. Britney Spears?

"That's ' cause you colonials are too dense to understand the finer nuances of the Queen's English," he said in jest.

"Ah, we may be dense, but we're tough sons-of-bitches," I said.

"You're a big one, I'll give you that. What sports do you play?"

"Football. I was on my all-conference team in high school. Even got a few scholarship offers."

"American football? See, you got to get all armored up for that. A real man plays rugby. No poofy helmets and pads. What position did you play?' he asked me.

"Left tackle," I told him.

"You mean, you tackle the guy with the ball?"

"No, I was on offense. I kept the defense away from our quarterback. I played both ways, though, sometimes as a defensive end, but my main position was on offense."

"I thought those blocking blokes were all big fat guys, like sumo wrestlers. You're a big guy, but you don't have a gut hanging over your belt. What do you go? A hundred, hundred and ten?"

It took me a moment to figure out that he was asking my weight. "In pounds, I played at 225. What's that in kilos, a little over a hundred?"

"Yea, thereabouts, I think," he said.

"Not everyone on the line is fat," I told him. "This was high school ball, and I was plenty big enough for that. I might have had to change positions if I played college ball, though. Maybe move to center, maybe switch to the defense. What about you? What sports did you play?"

"I played football, soccer to you, as a schoolboy. But I got into MMA as soon as I left school, and I've been training and competing while in the Army. I'm seven and three so far," he told me, pride evident in his voice.

"You've fought in the UFC?" I asked, impressed.

I'd started watching UFC on pay-for-view for a couple of years now. Those were some tough dudes.

"No, no UFC yet. I did fight in Cage Wars and Pride and Glory, though. I'll get to the UFC, though, right enough," he told me.

I looked at him in a new light. He was an infantry sergeant, and that meant he had to be pretty tough right there. Add in MMA? It was hard to say, but he might tip the scales at 170 or so. I was pretty sure I could out lift him, if it came to that, but in a fight? I was bigger and probably stronger, but could I take him? I don't know. When I'd watch UFC on pay-per-view, I was like every other man wondering how I would fare in the octagon. Here was someone who'd been there.

Rising voices outside our door stopped our conversation short for a moment, reminding us just where we were. We'd been talking about sports and some sort of Brit slang, but the reality was that we were prisoners with an undetermined fate. It was great to have someone there with me, but the bottom line was that we were both in a shit sandwich.

Dennis listened in, then shook his head. "I can't hear everything, but it sounds like one of them is tired of this. He wants to go home. The other one is trying to shush him down."

"Makes sense," I said. "I don't think anyone wants Kaseem to come back and hear that."

We both went quiet for awhile. I couldn't help but wonder what Kaseem had in store for us.

"So who won the World Cup?" Dennis suddenly asked. "Did we do it?"

I grasped at the opportunity to escape my dark thoughts. "I don't know. I was captured before the finals. The US didn't even win one match, but England made it through. I think they played again while I was in the Green Zone, but I don't remember who won."

"That wanker! One of my screws told me that Sweden and Trinidad and Tobago made it through, not us. I should've known he was fucking with me! I mean, Trinidad and Tobago?"

We kept on talking in that vein. I don't think either one of us really wanted to dwell on our situation, so anything to keep our minds occupied was a welcome respite.

## Chapter 23

*Iraq*
*July 19, 2006*

Gomer looked down at us, then back out the door to the others. I couldn't tell what his reaction was, but at least he wasn't running out. He stood there, two plates of rice in hand, mouth open in confusion. Finally, he placed the plates down and slowly backed away before turning and rushing out the door. It closed with a slam, and Dennis scootched over and put his ear against it to listen.

"I don't hear anything," he told me after a minute or so. "I don't think he's going to bring it up."

I let out the breath I hadn't realized I was holding. I had given Dennis the lowdown on our captors, "screws," he called them. I told him I thought Gomer might be at least a little sympathetic to me. We decided to try and put an offer to him.

Dennis dumbed down his Arabic so as not to give away that he was pretty fluent and basically said to Gomer "freedom us, money you" in what he said was improper and horribly accented Arabic. Gomer didn't seem too bright, but he should be able understand that. The fact that he didn't report that to the others gave us hope. We needed that idea to percolate in his brain. It would be even better if Kaseem smacked him about again, anything to alienate him.

Kaseem hadn't come by today, though. Maybe whatever caused my move and the bringing of Dennis made things a bit too hot for him. From how I described him, Dennis thought he must be Yemeni. He said the rhino horn dagger was the tell on that. Evidently, a Yemeni wasn't a man unless he had one. With all the demand, the rhinos were almost hunted out, and poachers charged an arm and a leg for the horns, so only rich Yemenis could afford a new one. Dennis called it a "penis dagger."

When I told him about how he had at first befriended me, Dennis told me that that was a typical method of handling prisoners. I'd seen things about Stockholm Syndrome on television, and our instructors for our work-ups had told us about it, of course, but when I was living it, I never really considered it. In retrospect, though, it looked like Kaseem was trying to set me up for that. His temper and his hubris (I never thought I would use that word again after studying *The Odyssey* back in high school), though, kept him from totally playing good cop.

While I told him about Kaseem and the others, while I told him about the mock execution, and while I told him about the video, I never told him that I had broke. In my mind, I had come to terms with that, but I was not proud of what I had done.

Now, though, we'd taken our first proactive step in fighting back. Whether anything would come of it was something only time would tell.

# Chapter 24

*Iraq*
*July 20, 2006*

Kaseem finally made his appearance again. He asked us how we were doing, did we need anything—the good cop again. He told us he had brought us together to make it easier to release us back once the US and the UK met his demands, which he assured us were very reasonable ones. He gave each of us some cold tea, which I had begun to view as the fish offered to Shamu down at Sea World in San Diego. I just didn't know what sort of trick he expected us to perform.

"He's dangerous, that one," Dennis said, after Kaseem had left and we were alone again.

I didn't need Dennis to tell me that, though. I had experienced it in reality.

"I've got a feeling that our time's running out," he said.

I didn't want to hear that, even if my gut had told me the same thing. But with Dennis giving voice to that, it seemed more real somehow. Kaseem was just a little too nice today, almost oozing with insincerity. Then there was the whole matter of bringing Dennis here, all the way from Basra. Moving a POW around the country was not without risks to his captors, and Kaseem's explanation was just so much BS. Something was up.

"I think I need to tell you something," I said, getting my nerve up. Dennis merely looked at me, waiting. "I told you that I had to make a video giving my name as a proof of life. Well . . . I . . . I did more than that, more . . . worse, I mean. Kaseem, he broke me. I said on tape everything he told me to. He crushed one of my balls, for God's sake, he . . ."

"Stop," he calmly said, "just stop. It doesn't matter. Whatever he did to you, he did to the shell of you, to your body. It means nothing."

"But I broke. I gave in!"

"We all have our breaking point, all of us."

"But you didn't," I protested.

"Fuck I didn't. They broke me, too. If they'd had a camera, I would have trashed God, Queen, and country on it without a second thought. I would've done anything to stop them. But they kept on, just because they could. They didn't want anything from me. I was ready to end it all. Bite off my tongue and drown in the blood. I don't even know if that would really work, but I was willing to give it a try. I tell you, I was done with it all. But then it stopped for the most part. And I knew I couldn't let them win. I could not give up. I was not going to be a victim."

I had been on the verge of a breakdown. I had been held for almost three weeks without someone else there for support. Now I had someone, and I was going to lay it all on him, let him absorb some of my despair. But when he told me he had been about to kill himself, that gave me pause. I wasn't alone. He had gone through the same thing. He understood. Now, here he was, refusing to be a victim. I had that in me, too. I know I did.

"The question is now what do we are going to do about it. If they've got plans for us, what can we do to interrupt those plans? Let me ask you, you're a pretty big bloke, but they've had at you. How're you holding up? They crushed one of your balls; can you still function?"

"The crushed one is gone, and the one I've got left is fine. I can't believe it, but my balls, or should I say ball, is not bad. My fingers aren't too good," I told him, raising my bound hands and slightly wiggling the fingers of my right. "They're pretty stiff and swollen, and I can't put any pressure on them. My legs have been shot and drilled, but I can stand, and if I have to, I can run. I can do whatever I need to do," I said, and as I said it, I knew that was the truth. I would do whatever I had to do.

"I think I'm at about 95 percent," Dennis said. "I've been left mostly alone for the last month. Physically, we're at where we're at.

What we have to do now is figure out how to get into a position where we can *do* something."

We huddled together and started going over plans, any plans. Some would have made James Bond shake his head as to their incredibility, but at least we were doing something instead of wallowing around in passive acceptance to defeat.

# Chapter 25

*Iraq*
*July 21, 2006*

"Well, something's up for tomorrow, but I'm not sure these three yobs know what it is," Dennis said from his customary position by the door.

Today was Friday, the Muslim Sabbath, and Kaseem hadn't come. We had faintly heard the call to the main Friday prayer, the *Jumu'ah*, so we figured most of the men would be there. But even after the prayer, other than the Three Stooges bringing us our food and water and taking our bucket out to be emptied, we had been left alone again.

"Joe is making the other two clean up, and he's talking about running a wire for power. All of them seem agitated."

"Another video?" I wondered aloud. If they needed lights and such, they would need power. They had some sort of light in the other room, but it didn't seem to be that powerful, and we didn't know what powered it.

"Could be," Dennis agreed. "Or it could be something else," he added quietly.

Dennis had confided to me what they'd done to him when he was captured. He was beaten, to be sure. But where they crushed one of my balls, they had hooked up his to a car battery. Not just once, not twice, but time after time. I really don't know which one of us had it worse. I might be missing one, but his might not even work anymore.

"Whatever they've planned for us, they don't want to do it on a Friday. That doesn't sound good to me," he said.

"Don't get too wrapped up around that. I might not be the Friday thing, but maybe they just need to wait for Kaseem to get here," I told him.

He didn't seem too mollified, though. For the first time since we had been thrown together, he was looking nervous. He put his ear up against the door again to listen. I just leaned back against the wall and waited. I knew the sounds would be muffled through the heavy door, so any noise I made would make it harder for him to make out what was being said.

"Someone else just got here," he told me. A few minutes later, he added, "It's tomorrow. Whatever they have planned is for tomorrow. I heard one bloke tell the others they had until morning to get ready. Blast! There is bugger all we can do about it now, I think, but we've got to give it a go."

"Want to work on our hands again?" I asked. We'd tried to untie each other's bindings the night before, but he hadn't made much progress. With my two broken fingers, I could only work with one hand, and even with two hands, Dennis hadn't been able to do much, either. The metal cable they now used to bind us wasn't locked with a padlock, but they had a clasp holding the ends that needed a set of pliers or something to open. The cables themselves weren't that tight, and we had a small degree of movement, but we could not slide our hands out of the first loop around the wrists.

"Might as well," he said. "I swear, though, if it comes to that I'll pull my bloody hands right off and beat them all to death with my stumps."

# Chapter 26

*Iraq*
*July 22, 2006*

Neither of us had slept well. Dennis being nervous made me nervous, and that fed back to him making him more nervous in a continuous loop. When the door opened in the morning, we both jumped, but it was only Buttface with rice and water. I tried to look out the door, but I couldn't see anything out of the ordinary.

"If it's another video, so what? They don't even release them," I said.

"They didn't last time for you, but who's to say that wasn't to lull you into a sense of complacency?" he responded. "If you think about it, you were pretty ballsed-up when you made yours, and that doesn't look too good on Al-Jazeera."

"I'll be honest with you, Dennis. I don't know if I can go through all of that again. I can try, but, well, . . . ."

"Just do what you can. It might not even be a video. We don't know."

I didn't want to dwell on it. We would find out soon enough. If it wasn't a video, what would it be? There were too many options that were just too unthinkable to contemplate. I could kill myself with a heart attack from stressing too much and save them the trouble.

We just sat there, backs against the wall. We didn't even try to make small talk. What was the use?

When the door finally opened, it was almost a relief. Buttface came into the room and motioned us to get up. He had his rifle ready and was not getting too close. We stood up and walked out of the room. Gomer, Joe, and another Arab were there, waiting, weapons trained on us. There were four of them and two of us, not too horrible odds, but they were all armed and we still had our hands bound. I was stiff, too, from sitting in that room for four days.

I looked around. We were in a large commercial-type building, possibly a factory. We were now in an office, abandoned and empty now. Looking back at our "cell," I realized that we had been being kept in some sort of supply closet.

Joe motioned us to hold out our hands. One at a time, simple handcuffs were put on us, then the cables taken off. That as a little strange, I thought. If they had handcuffs all this time, what was with the medieval-looking crap?

Once the handcuffs were on, Gomer brought forward a bucket of water. Joe motioned for us to clean ourselves. I was grateful to get some of the grime off of us, but I wondered what that meant. If they meant to execute us, then we wouldn't have to be cleaned up, right? We finished, then stood there for several minutes doing nothing.

Joe looked at his watch, then said something in Arabic, and out of the corner of my eye, I saw Dennis flinch, as if he was starting to move. He froze, and for a moment, I saw a hint of suspicion cross Joe's eyes. He said the same thing in Arabic again, but this time, Dennis just stood there. Joe motioned with this rifle for us to move, so we started to walk out of the office, down several flights of rickety stairs, then out onto what had been a factory floor. It was mostly empty, but there were scattered pieces of machinery parts, some loose pieces of paper, and lots and lots of dust. The high windows let in quite a bit of sunlight, more light than I had seen in several days. I had to squint to keep from being blinded.

The factory floor was pretty big, but maybe that was just in comparison to the small rooms in which I had been held. The vast room swallowed up the sounds of our footsteps as the six of us made our way to the back of the building. Just before we got there, Gomer pushed in front of us and opened a door. We entered to see another set of metal stairs. Gomer stood back, letting us go ahead. We went up two flights of stairs and were starting on our third when we were pulled back and pointed at the door there. This was our destination.

It was another video. One set of lights was already on, and the camcorder was on the tripod and pointing to two chairs up near the wall. On the wall above the chairs was a poster that said something in Arabic. We were motioned to the chairs, so we sat and waited. The cameraman had been waiting for us, so now there were five men watching us. No one said a word.

Joe kept looking at his watch, then walking over to the window that opened to the factory floor. We were waiting for Kaseem, it seemed, before we could get going.

"Notice how we had to move back here?" Dennis whispered.

"Yeah, so no one could hear," I replied.

Our other room had been closer to the street. We could hear trucks and such go by occasionally. But back here, we had to be a good 50 or 60 yards from the street.

The Iraqis didn't seem to mind us whispering, but we didn't have anything else to say to each other. We waited for what had to be another 30 minutes before Joe spun around and came to join us. It seemed that Kaseem had finally arrived. We could hear him climb the metal stairs, then come into the room, followed by his bearded bodyguard. He was dressed like he was for the first video. He looked around, then asked something of the others. I heard the name "Farid," or at least I thought I did. Even I could tell that they were telling him they didn't know where he was.

"He's asking where the other two are. They don't know," Dennis whispered quietly out of the side of his mouth. If my ear wasn't so close to him, I would never have heard.

Kaseem angrily said something, then seemed to take it in stride. He settled in to wait. After a few minutes, though, he came over to us.

"As you can see, we are taping this. I hope you won't have to go through the same things as last time. I trust you told Dennis here what happened last time?"

I nodded.

"Excellent. Let's just make this as quick and painless as possible. No one has to suffer. We'll get going as soon as Farid and Achmed arrive, so for now, please just relax." He turned and walked to the cameraman, checking the status of the camcorder, no doubt.

We waited for another twenty minutes, and I could see that Kaseem was getting anxious. He even pulled out a sat phone from his robe and looked at it for a few moments before putting it back away. I knew he wanted to call someone so bad, but with American monitoring capabilities able to track any sat or cell phone call, I also knew he didn't dare.

"He's wondering aloud if he should just get going without them. It seems as if Mr. Farid has a job to do for this little show, and if he's not here, someone else has to do it," Dennis said.

I felt a small thrill, a bit of hope. I knew what Farid did. He was the torturer. If he wasn't here, would this thing get postponed?

After another ten minutes, Kaseem had had it. He angrily shouted instructions to the others. I felt a sense of satisfaction flow through me.

"Oh, fuck," Dennis quietly said next to me. "This is it. Kaseem is telling the bearded bloke that he has to take Farid's place. He has to cut off our heads after we speak."

I felt my world collapse. Tunnel vision threatened to close everything off. Dennis couldn't be right, could he? He had to have misunderstood!

My sight came back, but still in a daze, I saw the bearded guy put his rifle in the corner of the room and pick up a knife that had to be 12 inches long. The edge looked impossibly sharp, and on the back was a wicked-looking saw blade. I'm not sure how I hadn't noticed it before. He turned and looked at me; I could see a deep sense of triumph in his eyes. Dennis was right. *This was it.*

Well, fuck them. I wasn't a lamb going to slaughter. I started to get up when Dennis put his hands on my leg.

"Wait for my cue," was all he whispered.

I didn't know what he had planned. We had gone over a million scenarios, but none really seemed realistic, and I didn't know which one he even wanted. I sunk back into my chair.

Kaseem told the extra camera crewman something, and that man nodded and walked out the door.

"One down. He's supposed to watch the front of the building and make sure no one comes in," Dennis told me.

Kaseem was walking up to us, all smiles. "Gentlemen, shall we get started? Let's get this over with."

He motioned Joe to go behind us. Once again, Joe seemed to be the speaker. He had stacked his AK up against the bearded guy's, so he was not armed as far as I could see. As Gomer started to move behind me, Kaseem grabbed his shoulder and stopped him. He took his rifle and dropped the magazine. He emptied it, putting the rounds in the small pouch slung over Gomer's shoulder, then put the mag back in and gave him back the rifle.

I looked around. Buttface was armed, and the cameraman had his rifle beside him, but that was all. I had a glimmer of hope.

Kaseem positioned himself behind Dennis with Buttface to the outside. Our executioner stood off to the side, arms folded across his chest, the polished knife point up. The tip of the thing reached up past his shoulder. Kaseem took two pieces of paper, handing on to Dennis and one to me.

"Dennis, you'll go first, then you, Nick. Don't cause any disruptions, if you please," he said jovially, as if nothing was up.

I wanted to reach up and strangle him right then and there. I knew the others would take me down, but not before I broke the little prick's neck, I hoped.

There were a few more instructions given, but finally, Kaseem gave the OK, and the camcorder was turned on. Joe was better this time around. He went into his spiel, telling the world about the Great Satan or whatever. I tuned him out. Surprisingly, I was calm and focused. I tried to figure out what Dennis was going to do.

In front of us was the cameraman, maybe 15 feet away. He had his rifle slung on a cargo strap hook on the tripod. To Dennis' right, the bearded bodyguard stood, just out of camcorder range. His rifle was a good 25 feet away leaning up against the front wall. Just off Dennis' right shoulder was Buttface, armed and ready. In back of him was Kaseem. He didn't have a rifle, but he probably was armed. In back of me was Joe. His rifle was up against the front wall, too. In back of me to my left was Gomer. He had a rifle, but now no rounds. Kaseem had made a mistake with that, but was it a fatal one? There were still six of them and two of us, and our hands were still bound in front of us.

Dennis had to go for Buttface first. He was the priority. Then he would have to go for the beard. That left the cameraman for me, but I couldn't leave Joe or Kaseem unaccounted for. Kaseem probably had a pistol on him, and that would kill a man just as well as an AK.

I knew I had to act quickly, but without emotion. I could not let anger or pent up frustration take over if we were going to have any chance of getting out of this alive. Actually, I didn't expect to. I think I expected to die here. But I would die on my terms and take as many of them out with me as I could. I was not going to meekly sit there while my throat was cut and let that video show that to the world. If a video made it out, it was going to show that they paid a huge price to get me. And if me and Dennis could fuck them up enough, they couldn't show the video to anyone. That would be a victory.

As I thought "me and Dennis," I smiled.

*That's right, Kaseem al blah blah blah, "me and Dennis." Take that English lesson and stick it up your ass.*

Behind me, I heard Joe come to a close. Out of the corner of my eye, I saw Kaseem nudge Dennis in the back. I knew then what Dennis planned.

It was showtime.

Dennis didn't say anything. I tensed up, ready to move, but I needed him to make his move first. Kaseem took a tiny step closer to him, then nudged him again. Dennis picked up the paper, then cleared his throat just like was getting ready to give a class lecture. I could sense more than see Kaseem relax.

"Good afternoon." Dennis's voice filled the silence, calm and collected. "I am Sergeant Dennis Coxen, of The Poachers, the Second Battalion, the Royal Anglian Regiment. I was captured in Basra on May 4th, 2006."

I'm pretty sure he was winging some of that, but Kaseem wasn't stopping him.

"Kaseem al-Gharsi, the Yemeni pitch and toss here, has more for me to say, but to that, I pretty much say fuck it. And to all of you ragheads here in the Sandbox, you can suck my big white cock!"

Upon hearing his name, I could sense Kaseem take half a step forward, then pause as if taken by surprise by the crudeness of Dennis's words. He shouldn't have.

Just as Dennis started to move, I exploded up with as much power as I could. I arched my back and led with my head. Even though I couldn't see him, my aim was true. I felt the back of my head crush into Joe's face. I kept going as Joe fell under me. I looked to my left in time to see Dennis' hand clasped around Buttface's neck as he jumped up and leveled a vicious Muay Thai knee kick right in his face. It looked like Buttface had been trying to swing his rifle up, but Dennis was too close, and Buttface went down. In almost one motion, Dennis spun and delivered a back kick to Kaseem's chest, knocking him into me.

I couldn't hesitate. The guy on the camcorder was already grabbing for his rifle. If he took a bead on us, it was over. The chair I had been sitting on had been knocked over, and it was between me and him, but I just ran right through it. My target pulled his AK and brought it up just as I lowered my head and slammed into him. We both went flying, his rifle skittering across the floor. He was stunned, and I didn't hesitate. I jumped on him and took his collar in my hands. I brought his head up, then slammed it back down into the deck. He groaned, but managed to twist and turn face down. I put my bound hands over his neck and started to choke him.

Looking up, I saw Dennis tangled with the bearded guy, Gomer struggling to get rounds out of his manpurse, and Kaseem getting up with what looked like a 9 mm in his hand. He looked at both me and Dennis, trying to pick his target, I guess. I didn't wait to see who he'd pick. I jumped up, dragging cameraman up with me. Somehow, when we got up, he was facing me. No matter. On the line, a tackle will always win if he has balance and leverage. He's got to get his center of gravity lower than the rushing lineman. I flexed my knees, got down, put my hands on his chest, and drove him. I heard the report of Kaseem's pistol, and my cameraman gasped, then started to slump, but offensive linemen know how to hold. I kept my hands locked around the front of his robe and propelled him across to the others, driving him right into Kaseem, smashing him into the wall. Kaseem's hand was flung back and his pistol went flying out of his grasp.

Below me, Joe was feebly trying to get up, but with three people on top of him, he went back down. I dropped the limp body and tried to get to Kaseem, but with my hands still tied in front of me, my balance was off, I stepped on either the cameraman or Joe and fell. By the time I'd scrambled back up, Kaseem was facing me, his rhino phallic symbol in his hand.

I risked a glance at Dennis; he was still locked together with the bearded guy on the ground. I wouldn't get any help from him.

"So, Nick, this is how you want it," Kaseem said, a gleam in his eye. "Too bad you chose today to die."

"Bullshit. You planned to kill us anyway," I snarled back.

I needed to be calm. I didn't need to get into a trash-talking contest with him. He didn't look hurt, and I was still tied.

"Ah, maybe so. But your death, both of your deaths, one from each Crusader country, would have served Allah, praise-be-his-name, so much better. It would have been so much more dramatic."

When he said "dramatic," he raised the knife in his hand and lunged with an overhead swing. I had taken MCMAP training, of course, and at the time, like most Marines, I wasn't that sure how valuable it really was. I enjoyed it as a sport, but modern wars are fought with rifles, attack helos, and drones, and most of us thought the whole thing was somewhat of a joke. When he lunged, though, something kicked in. Without thinking, instead of stepping back, I stepped in, raising my hands to guide his thrust up and over my back. His forearm hit my shoulder, and I swung my hands back and down, hitting him in the face.

With my hands tied together, I really couldn't get that knockout punch I wanted, but the blow still had to have stunned him. He stumbled a step back, the knife gone, and for once, that look of self-assurance was gone as well. I raised my hands again and stepped forward, but he got his hands up, and that deflected most of the force of my blow. This wasn't going to work.

I reached for him instead, grabbing him by the front of his Iraqi-style dishdasha, and pushed him back towards the wall. Stepping over Joe, though, I was a little off-balance and had left myself open. Kaseem reared back and kicked me between the legs with all he had—his foot impacting on the left side of my nutsack. I'm not going to say it felt fine, but without a ball there, I wasn't destroyed. With another step, I had him up against the wall. He reached up to grab my hands, trying to pry them off of him, but broken fingers and all, I wasn't having any of that. I smashed the back of his head into the wall: once, twice, three times, with all my force. He groaned, and his hands fell away from mine. I kept smashing, over and over. One eye burst from his socket, blood pouring down the front of his face, but still, I drove his broken skull into the wall.

I heard a clatter of shells falling on the deck, and that finally registered. I looked over to see Gomer was standing there, horror on his face. He had a magazine in one hand, and the shells he had been trying to load were on the floor around him. I dropped Kaseem's husk, and it slid down, leaving a crimson trail with bits of brain and bone embedded in the wall.

*Don't, Gomer*, I thought, willing him to stop.

He froze, his eyes as big as saucers. I just stared at him. Suddenly, he started scrambling for the shells he had dropped. He had sealed his fate. I was there in two steps. He barely resisted as I pulled him up and put my hands around his throat. He grabbed my hands with his and tried to pull them apart, but he might as well have been a child. I slowly squeezed. He seemed to accept it as he quit struggling and looked up into my eyes. Just before he went, though, instincts took over and he started to flop around, but it didn't do him any good. I watched the light in his eyes dim, then go out.

"Go with God, Farouk," I whispered as I laid him back down to the deck.

*Dennis*! I suddenly thought, wrapped up as I had been in my own battles.

I reached down and grabbed the knife Kaseem had dropped and hopped over bodies to get to Dennis. The bearded guy was face up and on top of him, but he had the empty eyes of death. Dennis' arm was snaked around his neck, evidence of the guillotine that had killed the bastard.

"He's gone, Dennis. Let go of him; we've got to get out of here," I told him.

There was no answer.

"Dennis! We need to go!"

It was then that I saw the blood, lots of it. A guillotine choke doesn't cause bleeding. I rolled the dead man off of him. The big knife that was supposed to cut off our heads fell away, revealing a huge gash in Dennis' belly. It looked horrible.

There was a gasp as he took in a breath.

"Hang in there, buddy. I'll get you out of here."

I felt panic coming over me, panic I hadn't had during the fighting.

He tried to say something, but started coughing.

"Take it easy, don't try to talk," I told him.

"Front door guard," he managed to wheeze out.

It took me a moment, but then it hit me. There was another Iraqi, an armed one, guarding the front door of the factory. He had to have heard the shots. I dropped the knife and ran over to the two stacked rifles. I grabbed one, took it off safe, then looked out the window and out onto the factory floor. I couldn't see anything. I was about to turn back to Dennis when the door started to ease open. A rifle muzzle poked in. He must have seen the bodies because I heard a shout as he rushed into the room. He never saw me as I emptied half a dozen rounds into him. I ran up to him, but he was gone.

Keeping the rifle, I came back to Dennis.

"Thanks, buddy. He would have nailed, . . . ."

I stopped midsentence. Dennis was gone, too. For all he'd been through, he'd been taken out by a fucking knife, of all things. Dead is dead, but at least he went out like a true warrior.

I picked the knife up and examined it. I don't know what I expected to see, though. I heard a moan, and that broke through to me. Buttface was making feeble movements. I stepped over and looked down at him. His nose was broken, maybe his jaw, too. Dennis had fucked him up good. Without emotion, I took the big heavy knife and slid it into Buttface's throat. He didn't even gurgle.

I needed to get out of the handcuffs. I took a step over to Joe, throwing Kaseem's body off where it had fallen on him. I started going through his pockets. That was harder than it looked, as I wasn't familiar with the robes Arabs wore. As I finally found the keys to the cuffs, I looked up and saw him looking at me with the one eye not swollen shut. I had thought he was dead. He seemed resigned. I reached for the big knife I had stuck in my waistband, and he never even moved. I stopped, looking into that unblinking eye. In the end, I stepped back, leaving him be.

With my hands cuffed, I could not get the key in the lock, try as I might. I couldn't spend too much time here, so I gave up. I sheathed Kaseem's rhino dagger and put it in my cargo pocket. I put the big blade in Dennis's, figuring it had a better chance there of not cutting its way out as I walked. I leaned down and grabbed Dennis, and with quite a deal of effort, managed to get him slung over my shoulder. I looked back, and Joe was still lying motionless, his one eye glued to me. I shrugged, then turned to leave.

As I started to take my first step, the flashing red light of the camcorder caught my eye. It had been recording this entire time. I kept looking at it, wondering what I should do.

There was really no choice. I walked up to the camcorder and stared into the lens.

"You don't fuck with the Marines," I said before hitting the eject and taking the old-fashioned VHS tape.

## Chapter 27

*Fallujah*
*July 22, 2006*

With Dennis over my shoulders and carrying the AK, I stumbled down the stairs and into the abandoned factory floor. I didn't know if there was anyone else, or if maybe Farid would show up. Even the sounds of the gunshots might bring someone to check it out. I moved to the far left wall and crossed the floor, unwilling to walk right out in the middle. I made it to the front of the building, leaving the floor and entering a small lobby. A smashed reception desk and a few broken chairs were all that remained there.

In front of me was a single, large door. There was glass in the door, but even unbroken, the glass was too grimy for me to see out. I stood in front of the door, wondering what was on the other side. I briefly considered holing up until nightfall, but I figured that someone had to know about this, and when Kaseem didn't return, people would come to find out why. Mostly, though, the real reason I didn't want to wait was that I just had to get out of there. I had to be free, and now, not later.

Standing there, though, I could see a problem. I was carrying Dennis on my shoulders, holding him in place with my bound arms while still holding the rifle. On top of that, I had to bend my head forward to help keep Dennis more secure. The simple matter of opening the door was problematic. I could put Dennis down and handle it, but I really did not want to do that. Maybe I subconsciously considered that as abandoning him.

Finally, I put the AK between my knees and while balancing Dennis on my shoulders, opened the door, grabbing the rifle back up and stepping outside. The first thing that hit me was the "whiteness" of it all. I hadn't been outside without a hood for quite some time, and with the sun overhead and beating down on me, with the white buildings, I was almost blinded. I couldn't shield my eyes, so I squinted, eyes watering and my vision limited.

The second thing was the heat. It was like walking into an oven. For a moment, I started to back up inside to collect myself, but as I blearily saw Iraqis react to me, I knew that wasn't an option. They were probably surprised to see me, but that wouldn't last. In moments, they would take action. I knew I was committed and had to move.

I spun around, waving the muzzle of the rifle at the men and women around me. There were only a handful, I saw, as my eyes adjusted, but it would only take one of them to cause me a lot of headaches. Some of them dodged about as my rifle covered them, but a few just stood there, mouths open in surprise.

I started moving alongside the edge of the road, up against a concrete wall. An old Iraqi had been sitting on a chair at a doorway in the wall, but he got up and moved to the center of the street as I came up on him. He looked surprised, but not particularly afraid of me.

"Get back!" I shouted as I noticed two men following me as I moved. I tried to cover them, the old guy just a few yards away, and to the front of me, all at the same time.

As I swung the AK back and forth, my movement kept making Dennis shift on my shoulders, and I had to struggle a bit to keep him securely in place. He started to slide off once, and I had to stop and fix that, using the wall as a base on which I could push him back up.

This wasn't a particularly crowded area, but there were now at least half a dozen people following me, even if at 20 yards or so. Several people had dived back into doorways as I came up, but these others seemed pretty interested in what I was doing. I think it was only the rifle that kept them at a distance.

Up ahead of me was an intersection. I had to make a choice. I had had a vague notion of finding a place to hole up, but with the people following me, I knew now that was not an option. I had to keep moving, come what may.

There was no rhyme or reason as to why I chose to turn left at the intersection. I just did it. I hoped it was the right choice. By now, my entourage was up to about 10 people. They were holding back, but for how long? In front of me I could see more people. I had turned onto a busier street. I knew I had to contact some Americans quickly before a full-out mob formed.

While the adrenaline had been flowing during the fight, I hadn't felt my injuries. Now, though, they were making themselves known. My right hand was aching as I kept trying to keep Dennis in place. My legs were not just aching, they were hurting. Each step brought sharp jolts of pain that ran up my spine and into my brain. I wanted to rest, but I'd seen enough *Animal Planet* to know what happens to the water buffalo when it does that with hyenas on its trail.

I did pause for a moment, looking forward and trying to decide where to go. I could see more people ahead, and most seem to stop and notice me, what with the small mob now following in my trace. It would only take one angry man with a weapon to end this all. I wasn't sure how many rounds were in my mag, but not enough, that was for sure.

When I looked back again, the mob was slowly parting. I turned to face what was coming, AK at the ready. A beat-up car pushed through, then rolled up to me and stopped. It had seen better days, and I couldn't even tell its original color. Black smoke came out of the exhaust as it roughly idled.

As the driver's door opened, I got ready. If this was it, I was not going to go meekly. A 40-something man got out, dressed in the uniform of the police. He hitched up his pants, then walked up to me. With his mustache, he looked like Saddam himself.

Most of the Marines I knew didn't trust the police. Too many Marines and soldiers had come under fire from these supposed allies, and we were sure many of them worked for Al Qaeda or Sadr's Shia. My instincts screamed at me to open fire, but I knew that would be the end of me. The hyenas would close in and take me down. I withheld my fire as he came up to me and stood there, arms on his hips, first staring at me, then slowly turning to look at the expectant crowd. He looked back at me, expressionless, ignoring the weapon that I had trained on him. He said something to me in Arabic, something about his tone making it seem like a question.

"Corporal Nicholas Xenakis, United States Marine Corps," I told him, figuring that the fact I was an American was pretty obvious.

He stood there a moment longer, then said something else to me. I couldn't understand a word, so I just stood there. He repeated it, but I had no idea what he wanted.

"Go into car," a woman in the growing crowd said in broken English.

*Into the car with him? So he could make me disappear?*

I hesitated. Refusing him wouldn't go over well. He was a cop after all, standing in front of his countrymen. But going with him could have drastic consequences, too, anything from being back in captivity to a quick execution.

He repeated his sentence, a bit of anger showing through. I knew I had to make my choice. I already knew I really didn't have a choice, though. I had no options. I couldn't take him and the mob on, not with only one weapon. I could take him down and probably some others, but I would be torn apart by the rest. I lowered my weapon and walked to the car. He watched me for a few seconds, then turned and preceded me, opening up the back seat door. I walked up and bent over to lower Dennis into the seat. My leg almost collapsed, but I managed to keep upright and get him in. I had to clamber in after him, pushing his legs so there was room for me.

There wasn't much leg room in the back of the beat-up car, but still, I sort of collapsed back there. Dennis' blood began to ooze out onto the vinyl seat, making it slick, but with the back of the front seat jammed against my knees, I was able to hold my position. My adrenaline was long gone, and I was mentally and physically defeated. As the cop got into the driver's seat and got the car into gear, I was glad, in a way, that it would all be over soon, one way or the other. I just had to wait awhile longer to find out how.

The car made its way through the people, and as we cleared them, he picked up speed again. I watched out the window as we drove, seeing Iraqis going about their daily lives. I couldn't help but wonder if their lives were really better, or if they even cared. Saddam was a monster, to be sure, but now the Sunnis and the Shia were killing each other in pretty big numbers. Bombs went off in markets. The economy was dead.

As I stared out the window, something clicked. I recognized this place. We were in Fallujah! I bet I had been here the entire time. For a moment, I felt my hope return. I wondered if I could jump out of the car and run. If I could hide out, Marines would have to come patrolling by eventually. I tensed, my body getting ready for action. I looked up to see what my cop was doing, and then I realized something else. I recognized the place because it was by the government compound. The front entrance to the compound was right in front of us, and the cop was slowing down. He turned in where the several Iraqi police and two Marines were standing sentry.

He rolled down the window to present his credentials as one cop came up. I felt weak. I couldn't even cry out, but the guard either reacted to what my cop said or because he saw me and Dennis in the back. He cried out in Arabic, then motioned to one of the Marines.

"Holy shit!" the Marine said as he took me in. "Get the sergeant of the guard now!" he shouted as he pulled open the door.

I just wanted to get inside the compound. I wanted to be among my own.

"Corporal Nicholas Xenakis, United States Marine Corps," I said for the second time in 10 minutes. "I'm back."

# Chapter 28

*Camp Fallujah*
*July 22, 2006*

"We all prayed for you, Nick," Father Trent told me as Lieutenant Richmond nodded in agreement. "It's great to see our prayers answered."

After my unexpected arrival at the government compound, I had been rushed back to camp and to the hospital. There had been a small crowd there, waiting for me. The medical people wouldn't let anyone approach me, but I heard voices cry out their welcome, voices I recognized. Tears had come to my eyes as I realized it really was over.

The battalion CO had stuck his head in my examining room, but even he was chased away as several doctors went over me with a fine-tooth comb, and they decided I needed cutting. While they were prepping me, I asked for a cold Dr. Pepper, and one doctor was adamant that I couldn't have anything until after the surgery, but Doc Whipple, the same one who treated me when I was here the first time, relented and told me I could have one swallow. A corpsman was sent to get one, and I was given a very small cup with a swallow or two in it. Somehow, feeling it go down my throat was one of the most intense feelings I'd experienced. It cemented the fact that I was no longer a POW.

I was wheeled into surgery, and within moments, I was out of it. I wasn't sure how long it was before I woke up, but instantly, several doctors were there checking me out. Doc Whipple told me that they had cleaned out my wounds, but I would need some more surgery on my fingers, and they might want to do some microsurgery on my nutsack. They were going to keep me under observation for a day or two, then medivac me to Germany. The doctors up there would figure out what to do next.

Once the docs were done with me, the parade started. The battalion CO came in to shake my hand and tell me that he was glad I was back. The battery commander said pretty much the same thing, adding that they had never given up hope, that the Marines had sent out patrol after patrol to try and find me. It was only then that I found out that Tony had made it. Left for dead by the Iraqis, he was found probably moments after I had been taken away. It had been nip and tuck there for awhile, but he was back at Bethesda now, looking forward to getting transferred back to the Wounded Warrior Battalion at Pendleton.

That piece of information took away a black cloud that had been affecting my soul. I could not have heard better news.

Another bit of news was that I found the reason why Farid hadn't been at the taping and beheading. He and the other guy were picked up by a Marine patrol, almost certainly on their way to the factory. If either one of them had made it there, well, I think things would have turned out quite differently.

With the sergeant major, all the officers, most of whom I didn't even know, making their way to see me, I wished I could see my friends, my fellow NCO's and enlisted. Brent most of all, but Fowler, Harris, Blount, Hansen, Kim, and the rest. But the big dogs had to have their say, first. Down to the chaplain, the platoon commander, and Gunny Pancoast, I knew it was getting closer to those I really wanted to see.

Until the biggest dog came in.

"Attention on deck!" the shout came out.

"At ease," I heard before I could move.

The commanding general walked in and up to my bed.

"You don't fuck with the Marines?" he quietly asked.

I looked at him confused. What was he talking about?

He must have seen the confusion on my face as he added, "You really said that?"

Then it hit me. I had said that, or something like that, on the video after the fight. They must have taken it out of my utility trou when I got to the hospital. He couldn't blame me for that, right? Then I saw the big smile on his face.

"That was pretty impressive, there, Corporal. I have to say, I've never seen anything quite like it. Some of us have watched it a dozen times now. You've made us proud."

I didn't say I was just trying to survive, but that's all it was. And Dennis didn't survive. He made the first move, and because of that, I was here now.

"Uh, about Dennis, sir?" I started.

"Oh, Sergeant Coxen's body has been flown back to Basra. The Brits have expressed their gratitude. We're making a copy of the tape to send to them so they'll know that he went out as a warrior."

"What about, sir, I mean, what about the rest of the tape?" I asked.

I knew that the camcorder was the same one they had used to tape me giving my confession, blabbing about anything they asked. That was hanging over me. I broke, and I was sure that the tape I took also showed that.

"The rest of the tape? There wasn't any rest of the tape," he replied.

"But . . ."

"Corporal Xenakis, I think you must have taken a knock on the head today, questioning your commanding general. There was no more to the tape. There might have been more, but the tape was damaged, and that part was corrupted. Whatever was there is gone. It never happened because I say it never happened. *Capisce?*"

I looked up at him as he stood over me. He had a serious look on his face, but I could see the concern. I knew then that he had seen what I had feared, but that he had taken care of it. I still felt the shame, but no one else but him and some people on his staff would know. I guess even generals took care of their troops.

"*Capisce*, sir," I said.

"Good, then. Well, the sergeant major has a few words for you, but I've got to get back to the war. We're really glad you're back, and so's your family. We've got a phone coming in here, and I want you to call them and let them know you're still kicking. And after that, it looks like half the camp is outside waiting to come and say hello. Sergeant Major," he said, turning to him, "keep it short and then get the rest of the old guys out of here. I'm sure Corporal Xenakis would rather be seeing his friends than entertaining the entire command staff."

He shouted "at ease" before anyone had a chance to call the place to attention and strode out. The other officers and SNCOs milled about a bit, then made their way to shake my hand and telling me they were glad I was back. Outside the door, I could see Brent and SSgt Cordero waiting, along with what had to be pretty much the entire battery. I was tired, but nothing was going to stop me from being welcomed back by them.

## Chapter 29

*Camp Fallujah*
*August 13, 2006*

I got off the Black Hawk and followed the rest of the passengers to the "passenger terminal" at Fallujah. Strangely it was good to be "home."

This was my second ride in a Black Hawk. The first had been from Fallujah to Balad Air Base to catch a flight to Landstuhl. When I had arrived in Iraq, I had wanted to ride a Black Hawk, but that wasn't really the way I would have wanted to earn the ride given the choice. Still, even fucked up as I was, it was a pretty sweet ride.

At Balad, I waited around with the other sick, lame, and lazy, waiting for the flight. Most were soldiers or Marines, but there was a Navy lieutenant there, too, who had been hit by a rocket in the Green Zone. He wasn't like most officers. We all hung out in the TV room, those who could move about, that is, in our hospital scrubs, wrapped up in brightly-colored blankets made for us by grammar school kids back in the States. The lieutenant held a running commentary that kept most of us in stitches, maybe even breaking a few medical stitches when we laughed so hard. The guy had more stories than any comedian.

When a mortar round landed on the base maybe 500 yards away, the Air Force nurses went into a panic and yelled at us to get on the deck. We were watching a movie, so we ignored them. When one major screamed from her position on the ground that we had to get down, he stood up, calmly walked over to her, and told her shrapnel was nothing and didn't even hurt, all the time keeping a straight face.

When the major looked up at him and asked, "Really?" we all cracked up.

When he wasn't joking with us, though, he did have a serious side. I saw him quietly talking to some of the bedridden guys, holding their hands, letting him know he cared. I think he would have made a great Marine.

Somehow, people found out my story. A few made comments, asking questions, but most left me alone. I could see their looks, though, and I could see them talking to each other about me. I know some were dying to get the down and dirty, but I was being given space. I appreciated that. I wasn't ready to open up like that about what had happened.

PFC Chad Nesbit, though, rather broke my heart. Chad had been standing with his squad up north when a mortar hit his group, killing five Marines and tearing him up. His flak jacket stopped most of it, but his legs were peppered and his hand was pretty much destroyed. They had it in some sort of Frankenstein contraption, all wires and rods. He was going back to the US for more surgery. He came to me to ask me if I could do something so he could stay until his unit rotated back to the States in another month-and-a-half. When I told him I didn't have any power, he said I was a hero, and the general would listen to me.

The thought that he thought I was a hero was strange and more than a bit uncomfortable. I didn't go into battle without fear or volunteer for a suicide mission. I was just trying to save my ass. But what hit me more was this young man's fervent desire to stay with his unit, with his brothers. This was the core of what it meant to be a Marine, I thought. That hit me hard.

After a day at Balad, the big C17 arrived to take us to Germany. We hurried up and waited for about six hours, then sat on the plane in the middle of the night for another hour before they wheeled in the critical patients and we took off.

We had five of those patients on the plane on mobile beds taking up most of the entire right side of the plane. Each one had four or five doctors and nurses taking care of them. Several hours after taking off, one of them, an Army staff sergeant, died despite the frenzied efforts of not only his team, but doctors from the other teams. All of us watched as they fought to save him, and I think it hit us all when he passed. One of the nurses, a young girl who couldn't have been out of college long, sat down on the plane's deck and cried. I think quite a few of us felt the tears forming, too.

We got to Ramstein in the early morning, then were bussed up the mountain to the hospital, a rather pretty place surrounded by big, leafy trees. We were met at the front of the hospital by a host of people, then taken to our wards. The Marines had a staff there who took pretty good care of us.

I was seen by an Army doc and five or six hours later, I was in surgery. If he thought he couldn't do it, I would've had to go back to Bethesda, but he said it was pretty straightforward. Other than that, the Army doc thought the docs at Fallujah had done a pretty good job, so nothing else needed to be done right away.

I woke up with my pins in my fingers. After all that had happened to me, that was about it. I wouldn't be using my hand for awhile, but the doc said there was no major nerve damage, and after they repaired the tendons, all I had to do was wait for the bones to knit. By that time my nose, the bullet hole, my ribs, the drill holes, even my nutsack would be healed. A nurse even told me they could give me a fake nut, just like they give girls fake tits. I would have to decide on that later.

I only spent two days at the hospital, then I was transferred Pulaski Barracks in Kaiserslautern, a good 45-minute bus ride away. The ride back and forth to my follow-up appointments sucked, but living at the barracks sucked more. The permanent personnel could get in civvies and go out into town, but we were stuck in the barracks. We could sign out to go to the chapel, the snack bar, or the exchange, but that was about it. And since we were all from Iraq or Afghanistan, we were still under the no-drinking ban that we had back in theater. Here we were in Germany, land of beer, and we couldn't tip back even one. To add insult to injury, we had five formations each day, the first at 0600, the last at 2300. We could see soldiers coming back from a night on the town as we stood there in our uniforms getting mustered.

Luckily, I was only there for a week. They were originally going to send me back to the States, but I really wanted to get back to Iraq and rotate with my battery. I was told not only no, but hell no. I made my case to a gunny first, one of the Marines liaisons, and he got his lieutenant on it. I heard it went all the way up the chain in Germany, then over to the CG in Iraq, but the bottom line was that I would fly to Iraq, then a few days later, go to Kuwait with my battery and then back home. If they thought I was a hero of some sort, I might as well get some currency from that, and the CG came through for me.

I left the barracks and went to a warehouse they had set up for people going back in theater. There had to be 200 cots set up for us. It was pretty sparse. We had a big screen TV and a bunch of DVDs, and the USO had brought a couple of hundred books, but that was about it. We couldn't go anywhere or do anything. We weren't even getting out of Germany, though. Each day, we would check how many people would get on one of the listed flights, and each day, zero seats would be released. There were over 30 soldiers who had been waiting for as long as 17 days just to get back to Afghanistan. I was beginning to worry that I wouldn't make it back before my battery started their retrograde.

On my fourth day, an Air Force colonel showed up, just like the rest of us. He got a cot over in the area where some officers, mostly lieutenants, had claimed theirs, but he sat around with us, watching movies, waiting for chow. He raised a stink that we couldn't leave the barracks, and the Army staff sergeant at the front desk at first said that was because a flight could materialize at a moment's notice. When the colonel persisted, the soldier said that a lieutenant was caught fucking a female corporal about six months ago, so the base commander ordered all returning personnel be confined to the warehouse.

I heard mutters of "Big Army" from among us—of course, we were all listening in. The colonel said that was "fucked up." Yeah, a colonel, using those exact words. But he came back to us and took a seat to watch *Shrek 2*.

The next morning, there were two flights that supposedly had seats, so about 25 of us were bussed to Ramstein, and there we waited. About two hours before the flights were to leave, those seats disappeared. The colonel went off, storming to the passenger counter and let the poor civilian there have it. We crowded around in back of him. The civilian tried to explain that it was up to the pilots if they wanted to take anyone. The planes were mostly C17s, and since Ramstein was not a pax port, they could refuse passengers if they wanted. He stammered out that since taking passengers created an additional paperwork drill, most crews simply declined to take any.

Colonel Simms, that was his name, called us over in the back of the passenger waiting area. "We're getting royally screwed here, but that's why I'm here, to be honest. My boss, the CG of MNF-Iraq, sent me here to find out what was going on, and to be blunt, he's not going to be happy. This is worse than we'd heard, and I apologize to all of you. No warrior should be treated like this. I'm going to get on the hook with him and bring him up to date. I don't want anyone to go back to Kaiserslautern. There's another C17 leaving for Al Asad this afternoon, and I can pretty much guarantee that all of us will be on it."

He was a good as his word. He made his call back to Iraq. The crew of that afternoon's C17 still tried to zero out the pax load, but I guess three stars carry weight, because that suddenly changed back to 58 pax, and that afternoon, the lot of us accompanied some sort of aircraft engine back to the Sandbox.

I overnighted at Al Asad, then caught the Black Hawk to Fallujah. I stepped out, following the others to the terminal. I didn't have much with me, which was good as my arm was in a sling. I had my assault pack with a sci-fi book I'd taken from Kaiserslautern, shaving gear, a toothbrush, and the rainbow colored blanket I'd gotten at Balad, the one made by school kids. On the way to Germany, my pack had held my uniform and boots, but now I was wearing them.

Before I got to the terminal, which was only the size of a shack or something, I heard my name called out. Over to the right, outside the plywood terminal, Lieutenant Richmond, Gunny Pancoast, Gunny Templeton, and Brent were waving me over. I looked at the rest of the passengers filing into the terminal, wondering if I needed to sign something, but that was my lieutenant, so screw them. I peeled off and met them.

"So, our malingerer is back, huh?" Gunny Pancoast said, hand automatically out to shake before realizing my right hand was in a sling.

"You can't get rid of me that easily, gunny," I replied, my heart pounding. I hadn't realized I missed them, my brothers-in-arms, so much. I was touched, to be honest, to see the lieutenant and the two gunnies coming out to meet me, just a corporal, but I really wanted to see my friends, the other NCOs and enlisted.

"Well, we've got two more convoys before we leave, so I can put you to good use, unless you're telling me that that busted wing of yours means you're on light duty," Gunny Templeton said, giving my good shoulder a smack.

"You give me a vehicle, and I'll drive it back to Seal Beach, one-armed or not."

"If you three are all done, I think there is a little party planned, right, Corporal Cooperage?" the lieutenant asked.

"Yes sir! We've got some people mighty eager to see Nick back with us."

"Well, then, let's get going," he said, motioning for us to get in the Humvee. "No, I think you've earned the front seat," he said as I started for the back. "I'll walk back and meet you all back at the CP."

I pulled myself into the front seat. It was hard to believe that I was back. I couldn't wait to see everyone.

"We're really proud of you, Corporal Xenakis. Nick. Really. Glad you're back," the lieutenant said before closing the door. He stepped back, saluted me, than slapped the Hummer's side so Brent could take off.

I was really glad, too.

## Chapter 30

*Seal Beach, CA*
*August 23, 2006*

It didn't matter that this was my third pump or first. As the buses pulled up to the reserve center, there was a growing feeling of excitement. We were almost home. Families had put up banners and balloons at the entrance, and we could see kids and adults milling about, waiting for us. Several news teams were there, too, ready to capture just the right moment for the 5 o'clock news.

We had left Iraq almost four days before, being trucked to Al Asad, then flown the next day to Camp Liberty in Kuwait. While being in Kuwait relieved us from the ever-present chance of an attack, I think leaving Iraq made us even more anxious to get home. Our mission was done, so get us back!

We did not take Camp Liberty seriously. We made the usual catcalls to the newbies coming it with things like "You'll be sorry!" and such. We ate chow. We hung out at the gym or rec center. The first sergeant said the reason we didn't fly straight back was so we could "decompress" from being lean, green, fighting machines and back into model citizens.

We had to go through classes on getting back; typical stuff like don't hit your wife, call if you feel anxious, shit like that. OK, they didn't really exactly say not to hit your wife, but that's what they meant. They asked us if we killed anybody, if we saw anyone killed. We even had to put that on a form and sign it. I'm not sure why, but I didn't check the box that I had done any of that.

The other main event was to get inspected. It was worse than any airport back in the States. We had to unpack everything and lay it out for the inspectors to check. With my arm in a sling, Brent had to help me get my stuff on display. The inspectors didn't find any grenade or rounds or anything from anybody, but they did confiscate some souvenirs, even one from our lieutenant.

Finally, though, we were loaded up on a United 747, ready to go home. This was not your typical charter. It was a real plane that United used all the time. It had three classes of service, not that I came within spitting distance of even business class. First class only had the colonels and sergeants majors there, and business class was the rest of the officers and down to some gunnies. The flight attendants told us that the crew was volunteering their time for free.

We stopped in Ireland like last time, and I had my first beer since I left the States. It was mighty fine. We were all warned not to get drunk, but a few of us made a pretty good attempt at getting there before we had to board again.

Next stop was Gander. They had some folks there handing out cookies, cupcakes and fruit, welcoming us back to North American, at least. I thought it was kind of cool that the Canadians were so friendly to us. Maybe the big crash they had there, where all the soldiers died, built stronger ties between the people of Gander and the US military.

During the last leg to March, not many of us slept. There's something about getting home that really can't be explained to others who haven't served. I know other people go away for their jobs, but when a violent death is such a real possibility, it's like once you get back to your home turf, it's really over. You have survived.

We all cheered as the plane touched down at March. We didn't need to be told to get ready. We were all standing up in the aisle, waiting to get off the big bird. We filed down the stairs and into a hanger where we were met by old guys from the VFW waiting to sign us up now that we qualified for membership (I had already joined after my first pump), lots of snacks, and not much else. None of us understood why we had to park ourselves on a piece of deck and wait, and wait, and wait. How hard could it be to just get on a bus and get home?

At least someone was smart enough to have the food there. We all started to bitch at the delay, but it's hard to bitch too much when you're stuffing your face on a free Krispy Kreme glazed doughnut. Finally, though, we were loaded on the buses for the ride back. We had delayed just long enough to hit the traffic on the 91 when we reached Corona. It took more than another hour to reach Seal

Beach, but finally, we were back. We piled off the buses, and there was a mad rush of bodies as husbands and wives, parents and kids flung themselves at each other. The single guys looked out of place as they just high-fived each other as mission accomplished.

It took me a moment, but I spotted my parents and sis. I had called all of them, of course, from Fallujah, and let them know what had happened and that I was OK, and I knew the Corps had sent someone to let them know I was no longer a POW. I didn't think there had been any press release or anything, just that I had been freed, and I had been warned by a public affairs officer that the news teams might want an interview. I didn't know just how much my family knew.

Actually, I saw Cali first as she barreled her way through the bodies to reach me. Cali was all girl, a rather cute one, if I could say that about my little sister, but she still had the Xenakis size to her. She smacked right into Captain Dorsey, almost making him drop his baby girl, as she rushed up. She had her arms out ready to bear hug me, but seeing my arm in a sling, she hesitated, a look of worry coming over her face.

"Come here, baby sister," I told her, my good arm outstretched.

She melted into my hold, her own arms snaking around my back to give me a good, strong, Xenakis squeeze.

"You OK there, Nick?" she asked as she pulled back to stare up into my face.

By that time, my mom and dad had made it through the people to reach me. With Cali still wrapped around me, my dad reached out with his right hand, then switched it so we could shake with our left hands. He didn't let up, though, giving my hand a crushing squeeze. I didn't let up either, giving as good as I got.

My mom just stood there for a moment, then slowly moved in. She enveloped me as Cali slid to the side. No words were spoken for a few moments, and even if I was a good five inches taller than her, I was her little boy again.

It took awhile, but finally, she let up and backed off. As the questions started, I looked around to see who else might be in back of them.

"She called, Nick, to say she's running late. She's on her way," Cali told me, knowing who I was looking for.

I hadn't expected much different, to be honest, but still, it kind of stung.

Brent came over to introduce me to his parents and his girlfriend. His father seemed impressed with me and tried to tell me about a couple of soldiers he had known in Vietnam who had become POWs.

"Come on, dad, you promised you wouldn't go all Vietnam on him," Brent admonished him.

"I know, son, but I wanted him to know that he's not alone. It's OK," he said.

"He knows he's OK, dad," he said while rolling his eyes before turning to me. "Sorry Nick, he just can't ever resist telling anyone about his time in Vietnam."

"It's OK," I told him. But that made me wonder just how much people back here knew about what had happened. I wasn't sure I was really ready to talk about too much yet.

We milled about for the next hour or so as the next set of buses came in. The CO and the I&I both gave us welcome back speeches. The sergeant major gave us his welcome back, all the time holding his two-year-old daughter on his hip. She kept reaching up to touch the side of his face while he told us to be careful about drinking and driving, that sort of thing. It was kind of cute seeing the big bad sergeant major so completely wrapped around the little finger of his tiny daughter.

The rest of the Marines and sailors had to turn in their weapons to the armory. I hadn't drawn a new one after I got back to Fallujah, so at least I didn't have to wait in line for that. I still couldn't leave though. We were going to have one last formation before we were dismissed for a 96. On Monday, we had to report back to begin our demobilization process.

It was at least an hour later before I saw a familiar figure searching the area. I had to say, Sig looked great. She had on a dark brown dress that cinched at the waist and showed off her figure. Some of the wives had dressed, well, I guess "trampy" would be accurate. I don't mean to be catty, and after being away each other for so long, I'm sure the husbands appreciated it. But Sig looked just as sexy but a lot more classy.

She caught sight of us and came over, taking my good hand and leaning up for a kiss on the cheek. She looked at my right arm in the sling and furrowed her brows for a moment. Was that concern I saw there?

"Sorry I'm late. I couldn't get off work, and traffic was murder," she said. "Welcome home."

"Good to be here," I told her.

I glanced up and caught the look of disdain Cali was giving Sig. I caught my mom's look, too, which while it might not have had the daggers coming out of her eyes that Cali had, it wasn't too welcoming, either.

Sig didn't seem to notice. She stepped to the side, but she kept ahold of my hand as she stood beside me. At least she did until her cell phone rang.

"Oh, sorry, I've got to answer this," she said, moving away 10 yards or so away from us so she could talk.

I looked up at Cali and tilted my head in the Xenakis family sign for a question.

"What?" she said back at me.

"Why the evil eye, Cali"

My mom came between us. "Not now, Callia. Nicholas just got back, and today is going to be a celebration." She turned to me. "Your Uncle Stavros' got a lamb cooking his backyard. He had to go all the way up to Bishop to get it. And your Aunt Rhoda and Kathy have been cooking all day. All your favorite foods: *avgolemon, lachanodolmades, paidakia, keftedes, moussaka,* all your favorites. All special for you."

Despite myself, my heart jumped. My uncle would BBQ a whole lamb, just like they do back in Greece. And as far as the other dishes? My mouth was already starting to water. *Paidakia,* which was just lamb chops with lemon and oregano, might seem like overkill when we were having a whole lamb, but there is no such thing as too much when talking about this kind of food.

"*Galaktoboureko?*" I asked hopefully.

"Yes, especially *galaktoboureko*," she said with a laugh as she hugged me.

My Aunt Kathy, whose ancestor came to the New World almost 400 years ago from England, my freckled, rotund, non-Greek looking aunt, made the best *galaktoboureko* in the world. The phyllo and custard dessert was maybe the single best thing the Greek culture ever came up with, at least in my humble opinion. Forget democracy, algebra, geometry, the Olympics. It's *galaktoboureko*!

I looked over at Sig. She was in an animated discussion with someone. I would have thought that with me just getting back, she could at least turn off the phone for an hour. I put it out of my mind and turned back to my mother.

"So, what else're we having?"

The food in the Fallujah DFAC was really pretty good. I had no complaints about it. But it wasn't home cooking. It wasn't a family meal.

Before she could reply, the gunny got on the bullhorn to call us to formation. Finally!

I gave my mom a kiss on the cheek and took my place. It wasn't a long formation. The CO took the formation and gave us a job well done. The regimental CO was there, all the way from Fort Worth. Our CO turned to him and asked for permission to dismiss us. The regimental CO stood up from his seat and gravely gave his OK. The CO did an about face and called the sergeant major forward.

"Sergeant major, dismiss the battalion!" He did an about face, then stepped off as the other officers followed his lead.

The sergeant major did his own about face, then looked over us before saying the words we were waiting to hear. "Battalion, dismissed!"

We all took a step back, then erupted into cheers. Brent almost crushed me in his hug. Even Krispy Kreme pounded me on my back. It was official. We were done with Iraq.

I looked over at my family, my dad beaming proudly, my mom just looking happy to see me back. Sig was off the phone and had rejoined them, and she had a smile on her face as well. It was good to see that. I hoped things were good with us. I shook a few more hands, then strode over to my family. It was time for a real homecoming.

# Epilogue

*Hard Rock Hotel and Casino, Las Vegas, Nevada*
*August 3, 2008*

I looked down at my hands, thinking how far I'd come. I flexed my fingers, watching them open and close. Except for two nasty scars running along the underside, they looked and functioned pretty normally.

I wasn't used to the spotlight, but that is what happened when the video of my escape was "leaked" on the internet. I was still on active duty at the time at the Wounded Warrior Battalion at Camp Pendleton, and before I knew it, I had news reporters in my face. Luckily, the Marines kept most of the craziness at bay. I couldn't even watch the video for some time, but when I did see it, I noticed that it had been expertly edited. Oh, it showed what happened, but not all of it. The video didn't show my putting the knife into Buttface's throat. It seemed like the Marines wanted the video surfaced, but not what was essentially murder of a helpless man. It wasn't murder in my mind; Buttface was ready to kill us, and I was still hurt and had to take him out before he could recover, but a whole lot of people might not see it that way.

So I had my 15 minutes of fame. That was good for my ego, but I liked the T-shirts that the other Marines and sailors (and two soldiers) in the battalion made for everyone. Across the front was emblazoned "YOU DON'T FUCK WITH THE MARINES."

Sig used the incident, though, to file for divorce. She said she couldn't take the pressure of "the press," as if they were stalking my front door at home. I knew it was coming. My sister and several friends told me she had been seeing someone or someones, depending on who I chose to believe, while I was gone, and surprisingly, once she told me, she wanted the divorce, I was OK with it. I wished her well (maybe not too well, though).

Divorce is a pretty big thing (it still wasn't done yet so I guess I was still technically married). But I had one more life-changing moment. I was back on active duty. I reenlisted once I was released from the Wounded Warrior Battalion and given a clean bill of health. I had left the Corps because of Sig, but with her gone, that reason was gone. To be honest, though, even if Sig had wanted to stay married, I would still have reenlisted.

Now, I was stationed as an instructor at School of Infantry at Pendleton. Pretty much all of the instructors were combat vets, some pretty highly decorated, and I felt proud to be part of that crew. Training Marines to stay alive in Iraq and Afghanistan while taking it to the enemy was a vital mission.

It was Sergeant Xenakis now, though. I had been promoted shortly after arriving at SOI. It was officially a meritorious promotion, but I'd already reached the cutting score, so I would have made it anyway. Still, getting those chevrons on my collar was one of the proudest moments of my life.

I received a Purple Heart with two gold stars for my tour in Iraq. I was awarded the POW medal, but that one, I feel funny wearing it, to be honest. They gave me the Bronze Star with Combat "V" for rescuing Tony. As far as the stuff on the video, I've been told I've been put in for the Navy Cross, but who knows what will happen?

I'm proud of the Bronze Star, even if I think it might be a little high of an award. It will, though, remind me of what a Marine does for his fellow Marines. The Navy Cross, on the other hand, even if it gets downgraded to something lower, well, I was just trying to save my own ass. I wasn't trying to be a hero. I just wanted to live. It seems to me that even the most craven coward would have at least tried the same thing. I simply got very lucky that for me, it somehow worked.

Tony was still in the Wounded Warrior Battalion, going through intensive therapy at the Naval Hospital, so we saw each there pretty regularly. He was still a Marine, but waiting for his medical board. He was probably never going to walk again what with the damage done to his spine, and his right arm was pretty useless, but he was already planning his "life after Corps," as he called it. He was going to start a custom silk-screening business that disabled veterans could run from their homes. I had a feeling that he'd succeed in it.

One thing that surprised me was that Joe, or Hammad Zobi, I guess his real name is, was given asylum in the US. I am not sure what Al Qaeda thought of him after I escaped, but after the video came out, his wife and son were murdered. Evidently, some in Iraq thought his "conversion" to the cause had been faked, and that he had helped me escape. He was not around when his family was killed, and he managed to get to the Green Zone and requested asylum. I'm sorry his family was killed, I guess, but I can't say I am feeling comfortable about him being here. I know he has tried to reach out to me, but I'm just not ready for that.

The best benny that happened after I got back was that I was invited by the Leicester Tigers rugby team to be there when they dedicated a plaque to Dennis. The team flew me over, all first class, or "posh," as they call it there, and I met his family. They treated me like a son. I have to admit that I cried when the plaque was uncovered.

I only knew Dennis for a very short period of time, but without him, I knew I wouldn't be here today. I owed him a debt, and my paying that debt led me to where I was now, sitting in the locker room outside the arena at the Hard Rock.

Dennis had wanted to fight in the UFC. That was his dream, a dream cut short. I was trying to figure out what I could do to thank him, and then it hit me. If I could convince someone to let me fight, I would dedicate the fight to him. I asked the new WEC middleweight champion, Brian Stann, for help. He was a Marine who won the Silver Star in Iraq, and he had won the championship in March. As a fellow Marine, he decided to help me, and the owners of the WEC (the UFC owned it now) probably thought of the publicity of having a man who had fought for real fighting in their ring. They agreed.

I had no illusions that I was a real mixed martial artist. Yes, I was athletic and strong, but so are all the fighters, and they had much more experience. I tried to cram in as much training as possible in the few months before the fight, then I took leave the last three weeks to go all out. And here I was, in Vegas, ready to fight. It might not be the UFC, but with the WEC being part of the UFC, maybe it was.

Brian had his own championship defense later on the card, but he poked his head in to wish me luck. I was nervous while being taped and while warming up, but when I was told to enter the arena, I was strangely calm.

I got a lot of cheers as I made my way to the octagon. I hadn't ever fought before, but the crowd was behind me. We went through the preliminaries, my banner not having the normal advertising but rather a photo of Dennis with his name and rank, with a simple "RIP" as the only other words.

I listened to the referee give his instructions, the same ones he'd given me back in the locker room. He told us to go back to our corners, then asked if we were ready. We both were.

"Fight!"

My opponent reached out and up with his right hand as we came together, and I touched his with mine. We lowered the gloves, and with a big smile on my face, the fight was on.

Jonathan P. Brazee

Thank you for reading Prisoner. I hope you enjoyed it.

If you would like updates on new books releases, news, or special offers, please consider signing up for my mailing list. Your email will not be sold, rented, or in any other way disseminated. If you are interested, please sign up at the link below:

## http://eepurl.com/bnFSHH

## Other Books by Jonathan Brazee

# The Return of the Marines Trilogy
The Few
The Proud
The Marines

# The Al Anbar Chronicles: First Marine Expeditionary Force--Iraq
Prisoner of Fallujah
Combat Corpsman
Sniper

# The United Federation Marine Corps
Recruit
Sergeant
Lieutenant
Captain
Major
Lieutenant Colonel
Colonel
Commandant

Rebel
(Set in the UFMC universe.)

# Women of the United Federation Marines
Gladiator
Sniper
Corpsman (working title)

# Werewolf of Marines
Werewolf of Marines:  Semper Lycanus
Werewolf of Marines:  Patria Lycanus
Coming:  Book Three

To The Shores of Tripoli

Wererat

Darwin's Quest:  The Search for the Ultimate Survivor

Venus:  A Paleolithic Short Story

# Non-Fiction

Exercise for a Longer Life

Author Website
http://www.jonathanbrazee.com

# Glossary of Acronyms

| | |
|---|---|
| 0311 | Basic Infantryman Military Operational Specialty |
| 5811 | Military Police Military Operational Specialty |
| 96 | An uncharged leave period of four days (96 hours) |
| Cpl | Corporal |
| DFAC | Dining Facility |
| EPW | Enemy Prisoner of War |
| Fobbit | A person who never goes out beyond the wire, one who stays at the Forward Operating Base |
| IED | Improvised Explosive Device |
| ITT | Interrogation/Interrogator Translator Team |
| LCpl | Lance Corporal |
| MCMAP | Marine Corps Martial Arts Program |
| MIA | Missing in Action |
| MNF | Multi-National Force |
| O6 | Designator for the rank of colonel |
| PRT | Provincial Reconstruction Team |
| PTT | Police Transition Teams |
| RPG | Rocket-Propelled Grenade |
| SGLI | Servicemembers Group Life Insurance |
| SMCR | Selected Marine Corps Reserve |
| SNCO | Staff Non-Commissioned Officer |
| SOI | School of Infantry |
| T/O | Table of Organization |
| USAID | United States Agency for International Development |

www.ingramcontent.com/pod-product-compliance
Lightning Source LLC
Chambersburg PA
CBHW071303130626
46556CB00003B/1452